INDIGO EYES

MAEVE HAZEL

PLAYLIST

Half A Man - Dean Lewis
Locked Away - R. Cit, Adam Levine
Mine - Bazzi
Be Alright - Dean Lewis
Someone You Loved - Lewis Capaldi
You & Me - James TW
Outnumbered - Dermot Kennedy
When You Love Someone - James TW
Need You Now - Dean Lewis
Say Love - James TW
Better Now (Acoustic) - Etham
Where Do We Go from Here - Caleb Hearn
This City - Sam Fischer
Robin Hood - Anson Seabra
Hard Boy - Frawley
Mind Is A Prison - Alec Benjamin

AUTHOR'S NOTE

This book is not for everyone and I said that to myself and everyone before even writing it. This involves many emotions and maybe there are a lot of you that can't understand them (which is completely fine) and I wanted to let you know that before you started.

I'm begging you to check the Trigger Warnings I have on my website.

Check out **authormaevehazel.wixsite.com** for more details.

For my grandmother, Maria.
I did it, Grandma. I'm living my childhood dream. Hope
you're proud of me and that you're smiling from above. Miss
you every day.

PART ONE

CHAPTER ONE
INDIGO

HUGGING a tree hurts more than I expected. Hugs are about comfort and warmth, but this is the polar opposite.

My left cheek is glued to the trunk, scratched and raw from the bark, as my arms circle the width of the tree. The funny thing is, despite the discomfort, I wouldn't have let go if it wasn't for the sound of someone coughing awkwardly behind me.

I release the trunk and turn around, praying to God this conversation will be over before it starts.

"Blue?"

Almost like a natural reaction to hearing that voice, my eyelids close shut. Suddenly, the decision to come out doesn't feel like a good one anymore. The cold seeping through my layers of clothing was enough to make me think that, and a fifteen-year-old girl mocking me only confirms it. She might be the only human presence I tolerate, but I can't imagine how any part of this situation can be anything other than weird for both of us.

With a sigh of resignation, I peel my eyes open, only to

have a smiling face greet me. I groan internally, not one for exchanging pleasantries. She lets out a muffled laugh, trying to hide it with her hand.

"Am I interrupting something?" she teases, scratching her nose.

I grunt in response, brushing mulch off my arms and cursing under my breath. "Yup." I chew on my bottom lip and my body slides down the trunk until I'm sitting on the ground. "It was pretty great until you came."

Without an invitation, she makes herself comfortable beside me, a sympathetic smile on her face. The blonde-haired girl tugs at her earlobe, sizing me up.

"What's up with you? You look like you've seen better days."

I scoff at her remark, taking a second to elbow her in the ribs. She pushes my arm away before it makes contact and grins, as if declaring a small victory.

As much as I hate her probing, she isn't wrong, I'm just not in the mood to get into it. So instead of responding, I shake the question off.

"What about you?" I ask her right back, eager to get the focus off me.

"Nope, don't even try to change the subject right now. We're talking about you." Olivia lifts her brows and points an accusatory finger at me.

"How about no?" I inspect my half-chewed fingernails and avoid looking at her, conscious of how well she reads me.

I make the mistake of stealing a glance at her, just to see her green eyes bore into mine. I feel something unravel in my chest and I let out a long sigh before responding.

"Not sure." I shrug as I stare into the distance. "Something feels off with Mushroom."

She takes a sharp breath, undoubtedly affected by it. Realizing it was a rude awakening that knocked me off my feet. Awakening to the possibility that your most treasured childhood memory and sense of belonging may go to rack and ruin isn't a regular occurrence.

The tree is the reason why Olivia and I are friends in the first place. I never could've anticipated it and that's not because I'm six years her senior. It's just a result of never truly wanting people around.

Nevertheless, she's not the type of person to leave you alone. She simply forces herself under your skin and never gets out. She clings to everything you love and does her best to fall in step with your life. Something Olivia did with me. She broke into my life and decided both me and my tree needed a name.

She calls the tree Mushroom, because in her eyes he looks like one, and if I'm honest, I'm starting to see it too. And I'm Blue because, well, my name is a color close to blue. Plus, her desperate need to have a nickname for me.

At first, I opposed the suggestion. I've never named anything in my life, and I didn't see the point of doing so, but Olivia has a way of wearing me down, giving me puppy dog eyes I can't refuse, so I eventually just stopped protesting.

"I'm so sorry," she says, pity wandering over her features.

Her expression stays pinched like that for a brief moment until relief settles, turning her lips up at the corners.

"My brother is a tree therapist," she blurts, widening her eyes at the realization.

I take a second to register her words, and the moment they do, my brows knit in confusion. "A tree *what*?" I ask, inclining my head, waiting for her to repeat it to see if I heard her right.

Olivia laughs at my bewilderment, having fun at my expense. She brushes a few stray hairs off her face.

"I'm being serious." She draws closer to me, her expression becoming determined. "My brother could help us."

A tree therapist doesn't sound real. Not even close to it. I've lived for twenty-one years and have never heard of one. This is absurd enough to make me question her sanity.

"So, you're telling me your brother is a tree therapist? What are you going to say next, you shit rainbows or something?"

She gives me an unimpressed look. "Blue, I'm being real. Trust me with this one," she pleads. I press my fingers into my brow bone, trying to ease the tension away. The effort is in vain.

"Okay... I'm listening."

She lets out a relieved sigh that makes her shoulders drop, satisfaction settling on her features.

Too quick for me to step back, Olivia's hands firmly grip my shoulders in a hug. Instead of prying her away, I stay as still as a statue. Liv is unbothered by my inability to respond to affection. She just backs away, grinning.

"I'll see you tomorrow."

That's a thing she does. Says one thing and does something entirely different. Sometimes her inability to see things through bothers me. However, it's a big part of her and I wouldn't change it for anything.

I frown. "Where are you going?"

"Don't worry, I'll be back before you know it."

She whirls around, her backpack bouncing on her shoulders. She pulls up her jeans, tightens her jacket, smooths her blonde hair, and waves before racing off.

I don't stop her this time. I just watch as she leaves, abandoning me in the back garden of the house that used to be my grandmother's. A place she never planted flowers in and left open for me to play when I was a kid.

As I sit up, an icy blow of air escapes my lips. Thanks to Olivia, I'm stuck with a question that will annoy me all night: are tree therapists a real thing?

CHAPTER TWO

INDIGO

He actually exists and he certainly fits the bill, if you can believe it. Narrow mouth, prominent Adam's apple, sharp cheekbones, and unruly light brown wavy hair that contrasts with his sparkling green eyes.

He's standing tall next to his sister, hands in his jeans pockets. I give him a passing glance, not wanting to show any interest. He may look like someone I would've had no trouble sleeping with a year ago, but I've had that crossed off my list for quite some time.

I move towards them, deciding that it's best to leave my rudeness at the door, considering he might help Mushroom.

When I come to a stop in front of them, Olivia grins in the creepiest way possible, while he warmly smiles and extends his arm for a handshake.

I do the same, minus the smiling part.

"I'm Elias," he says, breaking the silence as his hand seizes mine.

I nod, hiding the discomfort I feel under his stare.

"Indigo." As soon as the word leaves my lips, I take my hand from his grasp.

Olivia hugs me, and I pat her on the back. I expect him to say something about my unusual name or my eyes, but not a single comment about them slips from his mouth.

Instead, he says, "Well, let's see what I can do for you."

As Liv rushes off to the tree, leaving the two of us alone, I gesture for him to follow. He lets me take off first and then falls in step with me, his strong scent invading my senses.

"Livy really loves this tree," he adds, keeping his gaze forward. "I really appreciate you letting her come here."

The guy throws a quick glance my way, but I only shrug, hoping the gesture will communicate that I don't mind her presence.

After we round the corner of the house, I peer at him to gauge his reaction. He doesn't give much away. Only stands there, his massive shoulders filling the coat he wears as a swathe of wavy hair falls casually on his forehead.

The moment suddenly feels so personal. I only know Elias as a stranger, yet here he is in a place so intimate to me.

Elias mumbles something, drawing close to Mushroom. He lowers himself to the ground, gently touching the trunk with his fingers, running them along the bark in a slow back-and-forth motion.

I look at his sister, then back at him, utterly confused. Olivia shrugs, making herself comfortable beside the tree.

"He's a dragon blood tree, native to Arabia. I think you can understand why he's not doing well?" He looks up at me, waiting for a reply that most likely won't come.

Arabia? I mean, I'd never seen this kind of tree before, but I didn't think for a second that he wasn't from here.

I remain silent, not knowing what to say anymore.

I feel guilty for not being more invested.

"This kind of tree usually lives in a harsh environment." Elias stands up, watching my childhood memory-keeper as if it's the most interesting thing he's ever seen.

"What's your diagnosis, doc?" Liv asks, mocking her brother.

Elias takes a deep breath, scanning the tree from the roots to the wilting branches at the top. His muscular hands are resting on his hips as his fingers tap a beat that only he can hear. I can sense Olivia holding her breath, waiting for the verdict.

"It's not like it'll disappear or anything." He sizes it up and licks his lips. "But he'll look less... alive."

I exhale loudly then mutter curses as I pace back and forth, not sure who to hit first. It's either me because I wasn't more careful, Elias because he dashed all my hopes, or Olivia because she brought him.

As I'm marching around like some sort of freak and Liv is still looking like she saw a ghost, her brother pats Mushroom like a great old friend.

"He still has a few good months left."

Like that makes it any better.

Despite my best efforts, I can't help but think about what I could've done to make things better and I *didn't*. It always happens this way: you only come to terms with how badly you treated someone or something when there's nothing left for you to do to make it right.

I sigh. "Alright. Thank you for your help."

I know without looking at my watch that I need to leave to get dressed up. I wish more than anything to stay home and watch a movie or read a book instead of going *there*. It's not possible to hate something more than I hate having to make an effort for my mom.

Elias rises, brushing his pants before touching the trunk of the tree. "You'll be okay, buddy."

I gaze at Olivia, trying to figure out why her good-looking brother is chatting with a tree. I mean, I do too, but never in front of others.

"You all right?" I ask, concerned.

He turns his head, surprised by my question, then he pats Mushroom again before stepping away. "Yeah, speaking with plants really helps," he says as we walk toward the front of the garden.

"E is trying to make tree therapy a real thing. Well, you're his first client." Liv laughs a little too hard.

Smiling is her armor, and I can't blame her.

Elias pulls her gently into his arms and kisses her on the forehead. She relaxes, a small sigh escaping her lips.

"I needed to do a lot of investigation, and it's really hard to convince people that something they've never heard of might work."

"You don't have to explain yourself," I utter. I get where he comes from.

He nods, circling a strand of Olivia's blonde hair on his finger. "I'm sorry to be the one to break the news."

Liv kicks my leg with her shoe, and I roll my eyes at her obvious hint.

I nod. "Thank you."

"E, do you think we can stay a little longer?"

"We should go home."

"Please?" She gives him those puppy eyes, and when he looks at me for a *yes* or *no,* I know he'll lose the battle.

I bob my head as a seal of approval, and the noisy one hugs me as hard as she can. When she finally lets me go, I take a step back, knowing I have to hurry.

"Thank you, Indigo," Elias says as I walk away.

I turn back and smile in response, then walk into my house. I head straight into my bedroom, the floor littered with stray clothes. I push them out of the way and get ready for the night.

Let the show begin.

CHAPTER THREE
ELIAS

"What are you going to do?" Livy asks as I inspect the tree again.

I've never seen this kind of species in person, but I'm familiar with its existence. What's fascinating about it is the resin is red, making it look like blood when you cut it. This only proves plants suffer as much as people.

"About what?" I raise a brow and sit up, ready to go.

My sister straightens, brushing the dirt off her clothes. She looks one more time at her beloved friend, then kisses him. "About Ava."

I sigh. Long story short, Ava is my ex-girlfriend who I lived with in Boston for three years. And my parents kind of think that I'm in town just to visit them, not because I'm actually moving back.

We always used to come together to my parents. Ava loved them, and Mom and Dad loved her too. They were pretty taken aback when I got home by myself and there was no Ava in sight.

I've never in my life lied to them. They overwhelmed

me with questions, so I told them the truth: Ava and I broke up five months ago, living separate lives in the same house until I finished practice with a well-known doctor. The doctor is from my university and is basically a plant savant.

I told them the reason Ava and I broke up was because she realized that we were not right for each other. And then their faces dropped, and I panicked.

That led to lies flying out of my mouth before I could stop them. I told them I'd met someone else. And if it couldn't get any worse, I lied about her visiting.

Next Sunday.

My goal is to forget about it until I have to come clean, so I shrug off Olivia's question and hug her tightly instead. I've missed the kiddo so badly. It's been a while since I was home.

"I don't know," I tell her. "Unless I suddenly wake up on Sunday with a girlfriend, I'll have no other choice but to tell them the truth."

She nods just as Indigo's door swings open, revealing the woman herself in a long black dress with a daring neckline and a cut that accentuates her lean legs.

Indigo has a slim, wild beauty. Shapely thighs, rounded hips, and dark hair that hangs in long curves over her shoulders. She's a beautiful woman. And special. Any man with half a brain could figure that out.

"You could ask Indigo," my little sister suggests, grinning at the idea.

I open my mouth to object, but the person in question shouts something to someone called Enya, distracting me.

She notices us. "You can stay a little longer if you want,

but I just need to be somewhere like—" she checks her expensive watch, "now."

I shake my head and put my hand on Livy's shoulders, leading her back to our SUV.

"Do you need a ride?" I ask Indigo.

"Nah, a cab should be here in a minute."

We walk past the open gate to our vehicle. I unlock the door for my sister, then give her the keys so she can get the heating going.

I turn back to Indigo to say goodbye, but my plans change once my gaze settles on her trembling body.

Shaking my head, I step toward her, taking my jacket off. She looks surprised as I put it on her shoulders. I back away a little, watching my shoes like they're the most interesting thing in the world. In reality, it's just a way to stop my stare from wandering over her legs.

"I'm sorry for being the one that killed your hopes. I can see how much the tree means to you."

I peer up at Indigo, straight into her eyes — one blue and one gray. Although heterochromia isn't new to me, you can't compare photos with reality. It's my first time seeing it and I can't describe how beautiful it is. How *different*.

She agrees with me with a slight bob of her head.

"Well, I should get back." I jerk my thumb at the car. "Is it a problem if I come back tomorrow to run some tests?"

"No," she says, her gaze fixed somewhere behind me. "You should bring Olivia too. I want her to spend as much time here as she can."

"Thank you," I whisper, finally backing away.

"Right back at you."

That makes me smile. She did thank me a couple of

times in the past hour, but what makes it funny is that my sister was the one pushing her to do it. Olivia has always been respectful. I'll give her that.

I lift my gaze at the exact moment Livy opens the window and sticks her head out.

"Blue!" she yells, getting her friend's attention. "Are you free on Sunday?"

Indigo thinks for a second before responding, "Depends."

I don't need a genius to tell me why she's asking that. I bolt to the car, praying to God to get there and cover Livy's mouth before she says something stupid.

"Because E needs someone to—" I clasp my hand over her lips and she bites. Hard.

"Shut up or I'll hide Bunny." The yell-whisper works, and she stops her gnawing. I call out to Indigo, "See you tomorrow!"

I don't even turn to see her face. All I do is hurry, afraid my sister will blurt out something else if we don't leave quickly.

Olivia loves her plush bunny, even though she's old enough to distance herself from it. Dad gave it to her when she was a baby. But she loves torturing me even more.

Once I get into the car, I start the engine. Olivia waves goodbye and I do too, driving away.

"Why not ask Indigo?" tries Livy. "Just think about it. She's perfect."

I sigh, not wanting to explain why it's such a bad idea. If I were a kid, I'd probably think the same way she does. Seems like the best option is to keep up with the lie for now.

I'm an adult and that means I should've never let it go this far. It's my fault for panicking, and it's my obligation to make things right. Not now, though. When the time comes.

"E, please," Olivia begs, shifting in her seat toward me.

"Do you know what you're asking me to do? It's insane, Livy." I blow out a breath, trying to think how this might even work. "How am I supposed to explain why my girlfriend is not sleeping at the house?"

My parents will expect my girlfriend to spend the night because that's what actual couples do. They think she runs her own business, which is why she can't join me this week. *And* I lied about wanting to tell them first before bringing her home.

What excuse could we use, anyway? *Oh, she's sleeping at a hotel because it's inappropriate to sleep together under the same roof.* Yeah, that doesn't sound like bullshit at all.

Livy presses on. "Just do it and we'll figure out the rest together."

I laugh because there is no way that'll ever happen.

CHAPTER FOUR
INDIGO

I'M NOT the cleanest person on the planet. I've tried a ridiculous number of techniques to keep everything clean. None of them worked. And mostly because it's easier to find my stuff when it's all over the place. I have a way of sorting things.

This is where Enya comes into the picture. She's the one that takes care of the house and keeps me eating. She basically makes sure I stay alive. And it's not because I don't love food. I do, I love food. It's the best thing in the universe. The problem is that when anxiety sets in, my brain shuts down and fails to tell me when I'm hungry.

There are moments like this one when I can't find anything. Most of the time, it's because I'm overloaded with thoughts. My vision blurs, my hands shake, and I overreact to the slightest thing.

"Have you seen my blue hoodie?" I yell as I sort through the clothes on the floor with my feet, sweat sliding down my back.

The door swings open with a bang and the woman that

is like a mother to me sticks her head through. Enya is half my size and can read me like a book. "I don't know," she says, a knowing smile forming on her lips.

Her brown eyes avoid mine, even though I'm the one that's usually bad at eye contact. She's been trying for ages to bring me out of my comfort zone. She's not that subtle about it, either.

"Please, Enya," I beg, throwing myself on the bed.

The woman shakes her head and takes a seat next to me. She traces her fingers through my hair, my body slowly relaxing under her touch. Sighing, with my gaze fixed on the ceiling, I do my best to avoid giving her the explanation she clearly wants. Like I always do.

This is our dance: her trying to teach me how to communicate and accept people in my life. And me acting like I understand, but in reality, I never do, no matter how much I try.

"Please?" I whisper.

Enya nods, getting up to go to the laundry room. When she gets back, she's gripping the hoodie, which is as long as a blanket, in her tiny hands.

"Here." She hands it to me and I smile.

I sit up straight, pulling the sweater over my head. It covers most of my body and I breathe a sigh of relief. It's the most comfortable thing I own.

"Maybe Thory needs a walk?" she tries.

My head shakes in disagreement. I'm not in the mood to walk anyone's dog. Last night was a total disaster and a tough reminder that I don't have a place in my mom's world. But my mom doesn't seem to see, nor understand it. Indifference is her only way to cope as a parent.

"You can bring Kai and Nova," I suggest, knowing how much they love to play in the pool.

"I will," Enya smiles, then reaches for the doorknob. "I love you."

"Right back at you."

She leaves, most likely eager to invite her kids here. I've tried to convince her to move in with me many times, but it looks like nothing will work. Her excuse is that she won't be able to live in this mess. Bullshit. The real reason is she doesn't want to live in a house that isn't hers. All thanks to her ex-husband. The man was a real asshole, throwing his wife and kids out on the streets like he did.

Like I said. Asshole.

I jog downstairs to grab a coffee and some sweets. I like to have some whenever watching TV, even if it's a show I've seen before. Any movie you can think of is on my 'watch again' list. That's the result of having too much free time.

The doorbell rings, pulling me out from my racing thoughts. I take a deep breath and put a hand to my heart to calm it. It scared the shit out of me.

There's absolutely no way Kai and Nova are here already. That leaves only one option...

Not caring about my appearance, I open the door. Elias smiles, while Olivia throws herself into my arms, her shoulders shuddering.

"Are you okay?" I say. It's not a question I need a response for, it's just my way of letting her know I care.

She becomes still in my arms, not saying a word. I've known Olivia for four months, but that's enough to know she is all rainbows. Her brother does too. The effect her behavior has on him is all over his face. He's as worried as I am.

"She didn't want to come, but I thought it would do her good to spend some time with you."

I nod and open my mouth to say anything that would make her feel better, but I'm interrupted by Enya's kids' laughter. They enter the house, walking past Elias and stopping in their tracks in front of Olivia and me.

"Livy?" Kai whispers, clearly worried about his friend. They've met each other a few times, enough to create a bond. "Hey," he tries again when he sees Liv shift deeper into my embrace.

What happened? Nova mouths, and I shrug. My guess would be Mushroom, but it could be anything else.

Nova is only ten years old but she's wise for her age. While she's the smartest, Kai is the most tenacious and creative. They're opposites, yet so great together.

I step back from the embrace. Nova and Kai will take better care of Liv than me. The kids quickly take my place.

I lock eyes with Elias and nod my head toward the garden entrance. It's best if we leave them alone. I close the door behind us and lower myself to the ground, brushing my sweaty hands on my hoodie.

He sits next to me, and my heart starts to race. I'm afraid he might hear it. It's deafening to me. Second only to the sound of my erratic breathing.

I'm trying as hard as I can to keep my poker face. Getting used to people and allowing them closer is the hardest thing. You'd think it would become easier every time you do it. But it's not like that for me. Not at all.

My skin pickles every time someone I don't know looks

at me. My breath hitches when they close the distance between us. My mind empties, my hands shake and sweat, and I no longer hear anything.

On the outside, I look completely normal.

A blank stare is enough to fool anyone. You just have to do it right.

"I can't imagine being her age and losing something I find comfort in," I say, only after I'm sure my voice won't shake.

But I can imagine. I know what it's like to see things no child should. The only consolation is that Olivia doesn't have to live as I did.

Elias takes a deep breath, burying one of his big hands in his curly hair. I can tell by his body language how stressed he is. By the way his brows furrow, lost deep in thought, and how he rubs his shoulder. He doesn't realize how much he's revealing his vulnerability.

The guy loves his sister like she's his own child.

"She talks about you every day, you know?" The corners of his mouth twitch up as he surveys the garden. "Does she... I mean, does she talk about me with you?"

The weight on my shoulders lifts as soon as the conversation is no longer focused on me.

"Yeah," I say. And it's true. "She said how cool her brother is, but nothing about you being a tree therapist."

I didn't intend to sound funny, but he cracks a laugh, his gaze now piercing mine.

"Fair enough," he smiles, continuing to stare. His focus moving from one eye to the other.

Left. Right. Left. Right.

He must think I'm different, I know. Elias seems like a

curious man, but too respectful to ask questions about my eye color. Just as his gaze has lingered for a little too long, he sits up straight and turns back to the garden.

"I'm not going to stay long," he says.

"If it helps with whatever you want to do, you're free to come and go whenever you like."

He nods, getting ready to see Mushroom. He takes a few steps before I stop him.

"And, Elias?"

He turns, waiting for me to speak.

"Next time, you can go directly to the tree."

His face drops and I realize how badly that came out. I just prefer to avoid spending time with strangers. I don't want to see anyone I'm not familiar with.

I want to explain, but my mind empties, and my lips stay shut.

He walks away.

CHAPTER FIVE

INDIGO

THIS TIME, Elias dropped Olivia off at the door and left. I feel bad because he's clearly taken what I said to heart. I do anything to remove people from my life. It's kind of a habit now.

"You know, my brother is a really respectful guy," Liv says, raising her brows at me.

"And?" I say as I grab the remote and fall back onto the enormous couch.

After years of financial struggles, my grandma had all the money in the world and the best her wealth could leave me was her home. She had a big living room, large windows, an open kitchen, and a space dedicated to movie night.

We used to have a lot of those. She loved Indian shows. So much beautiful drama.

"And he always stops by to say hi," Liv continues.

"Uh-huh." Ignoring her, I turn the TV volume up, ready to watch episode two of a new series. There's nothing ground-breaking about it, but it's good enough to keep my mind from wandering.

Olivia takes the remote and turns it off. I curse under my breath, trying to keep myself calm in front of her. She is still a child, after all. And too damn smart.

"What happened?" Liv demands, turning her body to face me.

She has a serious expression that makes me mad. Eyebrows up, mouth set in a hard line, and arms crossed over her chest.

I throw my head back onto a cushion, a groan slipping from my lips. She can be *so* nosy sometimes. Especially if it involves someone she cares about.

"Nothing happened," I tell her.

"Nothing?"

"Nothing."

"Really?" Her brows do a weird wiggle and she smacks my arm. "I'm serious, Blue. What happened?"

"First, ouch. That was totally not needed, thank you. And second, this is none of your business."

For a moment, she looks hurt, making me regret what I said. That's exactly why I don't do relationships. Of any kind. They're far too complicated. You need to be careful with everything you say. I'm really trying and I still mess it up.

"You know I don't do well with people," I confess, waiting for her agreement. After she nods, I continue, "So I got scared and told him that next time he could go directly to the tree."

She sighs. "You need to go out there and talk to him."

I look at her like she's grown another head. That's the

last thing I want to do right now. Talk to him about what? He can't possibly understand why I said that. So why bother?

"Blue," she says, doing that little incline of her head, pinning me with her stare. "Go. I know my brother and he'll think he did something wrong."

I don't want him to think that. It's just that interacting with someone you don't know can be tiring and stressful for a person like me. It's like forcing someone that's scared of ghosts to play with a Ouija board.

I'm telling you: it's evil.

"No. *You* go talk to him and explain." I nod, proud of my suggestion, but once I see the look in her eyes, I realize she's not even close to being convinced. I try again, "I'm not doing it."

Olivia watches me closely for a few moments, saying nothing. That scares the shit out of me. She's never quiet.

"You can't be like this forever. It will eat you alive," she says.

It's not entirely my fault. I've tried, I'm trying, but things don't change overnight. Time will take care of everything. At least that's what I'm praying for.

As much as I don't want someone to feel bad for something they didn't do, if there's a way for them to find out the truth in a way that doesn't involve me, I'd prefer it.

"You gave up." She points her finger at me, almost brushing it on my face. Her features darken, her forehead creases and she can't make eye contact. "Besides your mother's events, you do nothing more than stay home and occasionally walk the neighborhood dogs. In what world will that help you?"

I'm trying to perfect my paintings and sell them online, too, but the motivation rarely comes. I only paint once a month and I never end up posting them.

It pains me that someone who spends so much time around me can't see how hard I'm struggling.

There's no chance she could understand. A step that's not even noticeable to her could be an improvement for me. It takes a lot of effort that no one can see.

I try to deflect by saying, "Whoa, Olivia. Someone woke up and chose violence today."

"Stop, you know I didn't mean it that way. Just go outside and try," she pleads, probably wondering if she took it too far. "My brother is perfect for you to practice."

I shake my head and get up. "Kai and Nova are waiting for you outside," I say, leaving her no room to try again.

Her sigh is loud as I climb the stairs, but it's best to ignore her pleadings.

She doesn't understand.

No one ever will.

CHAPTER SIX
ELIAS

Livy tried to convince me to talk to Indigo. She says she feels bad, but she can't do anything about it. How am I supposed to know what that even means? As far as I know, Indigo is twenty-one, old enough to apologize if she did something wrong.

The point is, she was just being honest, and I see nothing out of place with that. I respect it, even though I don't know what I ever did to her.

I sit up straight, brushing the dirt off my clothes, ready to end the day. I tried to get as much work done as I could, so it's pretty late.

Knowing full well I'm acting like a child, I call Livy on my mobile. I want her to meet me at the car, as I don't want to bother Indigo more than necessary.

On the first attempt, I get voicemail. Same for the second. I try once more, cursing under my breath as this, too, goes unanswered.

There's no excuse for her not answering the phone, so she'd better be dead or unconscious. It's the only rule I begged her to follow. Always answer if I call. Nothing else.

Although Olivia is still a child, she often behaves like an adult. The idea of her growing up frightens me. Mostly because I know how much I missed parts of her childhood while I was away. For me, it feels like every month she's celebrating another birthday. That scares me, seeing how fast she's growing.

One of my biggest regrets is that I didn't spend more time here. Studying and working for my dreams made me blind to what really mattered, stealing time that should've been for my family and girlfriend.

I guess that's why I'm not blaming Ava. She spent half our relationship with a workaholic whose attraction to her slowly faded. We both had a hand in how it ended.

Shoving the phone into my jeans pocket, I knock on the door. The wait feels like an eternity, but I'm finally greeted by a short woman with a radiant smile.

"Good evening, I'm Elias," I say and shake her hand, trying not to show how uncomfortable I am.

"Enya. Why don't you come inside for a second? You must be Olivia's brother."

Her smile doesn't falter as her dark eyes size me up. The black-haired woman cracks the door open just enough to allow me to squeeze through, then closes it behind me.

"She's asleep, but I'll wake her in a minute."

My gaze wanders around the big room. It has a high ceiling and bright white walls. I can't deny how beautiful it is.

"One moment." She raises a finger, letting me know she'll be back soon.

I stop her to ask where the bathroom is and she points down the hall.

Even the smell is rich in this house, but everything seems too quiet. Lonely. It's not what I'm used to. At home, I'm around my sister, cousins, parents, or other relatives. I'd be sad to live in a place like this.

Swinging the bathroom door open, I feel relieved to see the sink is nice and clean. She has a soap dispenser and a drying machine, but I opt for the hand towel. A documentary proved that it's a lot better to dry your hands naturally or with a towel. The device will bring back all the bacteria you just washed off.

After I'm done washing them for exactly thirteen seconds, I get back to the living room. A sleepy Olivia walks down the enormous stairs. She'll get her ass kicked for not answering my call.

I put my hands in my pockets and wait for her. "Rule number one?" I say.

"Always answer the phone." She rolls her eyes.

"And what did you do?"

"Broke the golden rule."

I nod, placing her head on my chest and kissing it. Sometimes I feel like I'm acting more like a father than a brother. As much as I hate it, I can't help but worry about her. If I say nothing, she'll do it again. And again. Until I have a damn heart attack.

Two voices interrupt us before I can say anything else. Indigo and Enya are walking down the stairs, talking about something.

I clear my throat, getting Indigo's attention. She presses her lips together, avoiding eye contact as they stop a few steps away. Indigo continues to ignore me and crosses her arms over her chest, hugging herself and unconsciously pressing her breasts together.

I swallow. "I'm here just to grab Livy," I say. "Sorry for staying this late."

It would've been weird to stay quiet, waiting for her to speak first. I'm the one who got caught up in work and lost track of time.

Indigo nods, pulling her fingers through her hair and throwing a quick glance my way.

"Don't worry about it," Enya dismisses, grinning at me.

It feels hard to breathe as Indigo raises her eyes to mine. She's intimidating enough when she's looking elsewhere. Imagine the effect they have when tracing me from head to toe.

Livy kicks her friend's leg, but I resist the temptation to laugh and instead act like I didn't see anything.

"Yeah."

That's the only word Indigo says. I find it funny how uncomfortable I make her feel, although I don't know what I did to make her feel this way. I try to avoid asking people too many personal questions. It's difficult to understand where she's coming from.

Indigo has the same blue hoodie I saw her in the other day, and a messy bun on top of her head. It doesn't take a lot to see she's a different person when she's alone compared to when she goes out.

"Alright." Enya breaks the silence, clasping her hands together. "Are you guys coming again tomorrow? I'm making Olivia's favorite cookies."

"Ooh, yes please!" Livy says.

The woman chuckles, patting the little one on the head.

We walk towards the door, Enya following us.

"Forgive Indigo," the woman whispers, her eyes winning me over in an instant. "Give her some time to adjust to you." She gives me a warm smile as I watch Indigo go back upstairs.

Indigo's not even trying to look elegant, yet she's the most graceful woman I've ever seen, looking ethereal in the dim light. The hoodie she's wearing doesn't lessen her femininity.

CHAPTER SEVEN
INDIGO

"I SAID I'M SORRY, OKAY?" Olivia whispers.

My shoulders drop with a sigh. Being mad at her is the last thing I ever wanted. I don't like it. Feels weird.

I know she's right. She's made me rethink my whole life, including whether I'm actually trying as much as I tell myself I am.

Going to a few charity parties a month and occasionally walking dogs is a good first step, sure, but I've been doing it for years and have gotten no further. It's still challenging. Every hour I'm away from home feels like I'm eating pickles. And I *loathe* pickles.

Yet, looking back, I've made no progress. My social life is practically nonexistent. Probably the reason the date my mom chose for me the other day ran away mid-party.

I was having a good time and didn't want to leave early for once. Turns out she paid him to stay with me for a couple of hours, knowing I'd be long gone after that. It was a little after two hours when he got up and left. Just like that.

At least Olivia sticks around.

"Okay," I whisper to her, hugging my chest.

She smiles, but it doesn't quite reach her eyes. The brief argument we had is still bugging her. It's all over her face. No matter how much she attempts to hide it.

I was once in her place, and it wasn't pretty. It got me where I am today. The knife that stabbed me three years ago, now twists in the wound my grandmother's death left me with.

Liv slowly blinks as she watches me. "Can you just listen to me for a second?" she asks and I nod, getting comfortable on the couch. Olivia does the same, readjusting her position. "You need to get out more."

I open my mouth to say something, but she stops me. "I don't know what you're going through, so I'm not going to push you," she says, taking my arm in hers and stroking it, "but I care about you."

I nod my head in agreement. I can tell she cares. She's such an extrovert, it's impossible not to notice. She always shows her feelings. It used to irritate me. Don't know what happened, but that's not the case anymore.

"I just... don't know where to start," I reply.

Confessing is harder than it seems. And not because of Olivia. It's because I've never had someone to confide in before. Enya tried to make me open up a few times. It worked, but not entirely. There are moments when I shut down and don't let anyone get too close.

"Come on," she says, taking my hands and shaking them. "It only makes sense to be him."

Without her saying his name, I know she's referring to her brother.

"And why is that?" I wonder.

She doesn't miss a beat as she straightens her back and spills out the idea.

"You've already known him for a couple of days. He's respectful, so if he notices something strange about you, he'll act like he didn't. And you're already getting used to him."

She has a valid point there. And because Elias is her brother, I'll believe Olivia when she says he's respectful. Can't say I'm comfortable around him, though. Elias is too curious. When he watches you, he sizes you up, shattering every piece of armor, searching until the only thing he sees is your soul. And he's not even subtle about it.

But what other choice do I have? Olivia is right. I know a couple of things about him, which will stop me from thinking I'm in a huge pit of mystery.

"I want to hug you," I tell her. I cringe at my own words. Feels odd. Don't know how to initiate it without making it weird.

Liv cracks a laugh at that, and she doesn't hesitate to throw her arms around me.

I CLEAR my throat to let him know I'm here. There's a green cup in his hand and I don't want to be the reason all his work gets spilled. That or I just want to give myself a little more time.

If he's surprised, he doesn't show it. He just places the container down and gets up from the ground. He still has his back to me, the rich outlines of his shoulders straining against the coat's fabric while he brushes the dirt off his jeans. It gives me a couple of seconds to gather my confidence.

Fuck it.

He's just Olivia's brother.

He turns around, the icy and withering wind messing his hair. Now he's facing me, my heart feels like it's stuck in my throat. Words get tangled up in a huge knot. I try to swallow to unravel them.

I truly want to say something. Anything.

But my tongue doesn't care. It continues to be stubborn and glues itself to the roof of my mouth.

His brows don't furrow. He doesn't seem to ask himself *what the fuck is she doing here, not talking*.

Or if he does, he's hiding it well.

"He's the best patient, so far," he smiles and when he does, the corner of his eyes crinkle.

Not having to start the conversation takes ten pounds off my shoulders. While there is a ton more to go, it feels a little easier to breathe.

I lift the corner of my mouth in reply and point at the utensils on the ground.

"Oh, those?" he asks.

My gaze wanders over his body. Tight jeans, a white t-shirt that leaves nothing to the imagination, black boots, and a jacket that enhances his arm muscles. It reminds me of the one he gave me, which I still have in the house. I should give it back to him before he leaves tonight.

Realizing how far my mind has wandered, I shake every thought away.

Instead of nodding, which I'd usually do, I whisper a

quick *yes*. It doesn't seem like my short reply bothers him. On the contrary, he smiles.

He gets down on his knees, inviting me to do the same.

"That's the resin." He shows me the small cup full of something that looks like red sand. "When you cut the tree, it looks like blood."

His love for plants shines through in every word he says. His green eyes lock onto mine as he speaks. It's almost like he's looking for reassurance or is checking to see if I'm still interested.

And I am. Not sure if it's about the knowledge he has or the way he's presenting it to me. No matter which, he's great at it. I feel like he's talking in another language. I only understand bits of the conversation, but it's enough to make me realize how important this is for him and how dedicated he is to fight for it.

The time passes with me delivering short answers and Elias wrapping up my grandma's tree in beautiful stories. Stories I've never heard. If grandma were here, she'd marry him on the spot.

She always used to say that plants love us back. I guess him saying they have feelings is pretty close to that.

We sit with our backs to the trunk of the tree, him looking at me and me looking anywhere but him. The conversation eventually comes to an end.

I try to control my breathing. The silence drives me insane, the need to fill it takes over. Not knowing how to restart the chat, I pick at my cuticles until they bleed.

My hands tremble, so I put them in my lap, but not fast enough to go unnoticed by Elias. He glances from them to my face, and I wonder if it made him uncomfortable.

"Who takes care of the plants, if you don't mind me asking?" he says, maybe trying to hide the awkwardness.

"Me." I take a deep breath, ready for him to tell me how bad I am at it.

Elias picks up a few fallen leaves from the ground and stares at them with those big eyes that remind me of his sister's. They are full of life, with curiosity glistening in them.

"You did a pretty good job." He cocks a smile and my heart goes funny.

Was that the same thing Nonna would say?

She was a lot like Elias: speaking with flowers, occasionally petting them, singing around them. Well, I didn't hear Elias singing to them just yet, but it sounds like something he'd do.

His effortless compliment has made me feel a little better about myself.

CHAPTER EIGHT
ELIAS

"WHAT'S HER NAME, SON?" my father asks from across the table, passing the salt to Mom.

The fork stops halfway to my mouth. My eyes dart from Olivia to Mom, from Mom to Dad, from Dad to Mom. I take a bite of salad to buy more time.

They took me by surprise. One moment we were talking about how happy they are that I'm back, then the next moment it took a U-turn. And what a turn.

Mom raises her brow. She's resting her elbows on the table with her chin between two of her fingers. I smile as I chew and point at my mouth to show I can't talk just yet.

Olivia straightens in her seat and shoots me a quick glance before saying, "Indigo."

I almost spit the food out of my mouth.

"What a lovely name!" Mom's eyes sparkle at me, and Dad nods while he takes a bite of his pork.

Clearing my throat, I resist the urge to kick Olivia under the table. Mom's gaze is persistent. It's glistening with curiosity.

I shuffle the food around on my plate, mainly to keep my hands occupied so I don't strangle Olivia, and try to think of a way to get out of this.

Things have gone pretty well between Indigo and me for the past week. We've spent time at the tree while I worked, no matter how cold it got with each passing day. We chatted about insignificant things. Most of the time, I was the one doing the speaking, but she was constantly giving me bits of herself.

My project on her Dracaena cinnabari (the tree's species) ended two days ago. Our meetings continued with me pretending I still had something to do. Couldn't make myself tell Indigo. Don't know why, but I couldn't do it.

She's slowly coming around and on top of that, she's a nice presence. She seems to love plants. Even the stories about my practice with Doctor Hall, that Ava used to call boring, interest her. She has a dark sense of humor and doesn't try to be someone she's not.

The shield she's built around herself is tough, but I'm confident she'll get where she needs to once she's ready and surrounded by good people. And there are a lot of humans on Earth. If neither Olivia nor I can get under her skin, there are tons of others that could.

I don't know that much about her yet. A week isn't enough to get to know someone like her. She's reserved, but at the same time, she doesn't have a filter between her mind and her mouth.

"How do you know her name?" Dad asks Livy.

She has an enormous smile on her face. "I face-timed her when E was taking a shower."

Olivia says it like it's nothing out of the ordinary. It

makes me question how many times she must've lied to us if she's that good at doing it. She doesn't bat an eyelid.

It's enough for me to get myself into a huge black hole of lies. Her pushing me deeper is the last thing I need.

Father laughs at her response, knowing how much this sounds like his daughter. She's always been like this. Slipping into my room, wearing my clothes, emptying my shower gel, using my cologne, stealing money from my jeans pockets. Nosy with an *I-don't-give-a-damn* attitude.

"Can't she come any sooner? We're so excited to meet her." Mom puts a warm hand on my cheek, watching me with her beautiful green eyes.

I shake my head as I put the fork down and swallow one more time before speaking. It's my fault things have gone too far. Olivia was only trying to help. She doesn't deserve to be dragged into my lies. Neither does Indigo. She'd probably freak out if she knew what my sister told our parents.

"She's not coming on Sunday, Ma."

My voice must express the shame I feel, because her expression dulls, disappointment flowing over her features. My father's shoulders drop the second I finish the sentence.

"There's–" I start, but I'm interrupted by my sister's laugh.

"This was supposed to be a surprise, but she said she'd come sooner." Mom and Dad's faces lighten as Liv delivers the good news. "Surprise!" She smiles awkwardly, looking close to shitting herself.

I take back what I said. This is totally her fault.

"Really?" I try to act surprised, which I am, but it's not a happy-surprised feeling, it's more like *you-are-dead-*surprised.

I unlock my phone, letting my parents enjoy the news while I text my annoying sister.

Me: Are you out of your goddamn mind????

I feel she is looking at me, so I stare right back, willing her to reply.

She sighs.

Livy: I know.

Livy: Let me talk to her, okay? I got this.

CHAPTER NINE
INDIGO

Enya points her finger at the TV. "Put that on pause and go walk Thory," she says.

I shake my head. "I'm waiting for Olivia."

"Take her with you, then."

She steps away, not giving my words any importance. It's clear she's giving me no option.

Since I agreed to talk to Elias and get out of my comfort zone, she hasn't stopped forcing me to do things she knows I hate.

Like calling to order pizza.

Hate that.

Hate that so much.

This week has been jam-packed with work-on-myself stuff. Nothing out of the ordinary for most people, but challenging for me.

Each day ended with a good crying session and an uncomfortable warm feeling. That scares me too, but I think it's just what happens when you try your best. Not that I'm at my best version, because I don't think I'll ever be, but it feels rewarding.

As the days pass, the feeling of knowing I did something good is stronger than the anxiety. Barely, though. They have a knife at each other's throats and are waiting for me to decide on which one I'm going with.

Sometimes anxiety wins.

A good example is when the delivery man rang the doorbell and I obsessed over the ways I could screw up something trivial.

Enya had to get it.

Had a little breakdown.

Cried because I thought I could never do this.

Ate some pizza with salty tears.

It was pretty refreshing.

Apart from the moments when the over-thinker in me isn't the one taking over, things have gone pretty well.

Elias is a contradictory element in my life. He's the one causing most of my uneasiness, and at the same time, he's the reason I get to do something towards achieving my goal.

And that is to be fucking normal.

He's easy to talk with, though — not that I do much of the talking. He doesn't invade my privacy like most people do (his sister included), and lets me be. In my own rhythm.

Even though Olivia is nosy, I must admit she's the main reason I got to push my limits. I'm not grateful at all at the moment, but there's a chance I'll be thankful for it when it's all over.

What stresses me out is people I don't know. They won't be patient with me when my brain freezes and seconds pass before I finally speak.

They love to laugh about everything you do: how your hands shake, how sweaty you get when a room is crowded, how you jabber.

And, if they don't laugh, their judgy stare says it all.

When the doorbell rings, Enya nods towards it and walks off into the kitchen.

I sigh.

I guess when someone takes a step forward, you push them to take ten more.

Taking a big breath of air, I get up off the couch and open the door to find Liv and her brother.

"Hi," I say.

"Hi." Elias rakes his fingers through his hair and Olivia just smiles at me. "I have some work to do today, so I only came to say hi and drop Olivia off."

A lump forms in my throat and I try to ease it by swallowing a few times.

It doesn't work.

"Cool."

And it really is. It relieves me to know I have a day free from the routine.

At the same time, I'm afraid that interrupting the only thing that's been constant for the past week will affect my progress. It's small, but not inconsequential.

Shaking my head, I grab a coat. The weather is sunny and crisp, but too damn cold. I step outside and Liv looks up at me, eyebrows raised.

"I'm taking Karl's dog for a walk," I explain as the three of us walk toward the gate.

She nods, looking pleased.

We say our goodbyes and the moment feels off. Can't

put my finger on it, but there must be a reason Elias is avoiding my gaze.

He gets into his car and drives away, not giving me a chance to ask what's going on. Don't think I would've asked, regardless.

Liv doesn't seem to notice. We make our way to Karl's house.

"So..." Olivia begins, hands in her jeans pockets.

"So?"

"Wanna know something funny?" she asks, the corner of her mouth lifting in a bizarre way.

Her brother's not the only one acting strangely today. I size her up, looking for clues to whether she's feeling hurt, because that's the only thing I can think of. Olivia is never this twitchy around me.

"I guess?" I half-shrug, not knowing what to expect.

She clears her throat, her breath steaming in the air as she covers her mouth with a fist. "So E had this girlfriend since high school. They moved together to Boston and all the great stuff. My parents *loved* her..."

She glances at me. Don't know what that has to do with me. We stop in our tracks and I stare at her. She shifts from one foot to the other, not meeting my gaze. What's up with people and eye contact today?

"And the point is?" I say, encouraging her to continue, not having any idea where this is going.

Liv sighs. "Okay, I don't know how else to explain this, so here it is: my brother got himself into a mess." She smiles and rolls her eyes. "Well, I got my brother into a mess."

Don't doubt it. "And what have I got to do with this?"

"I need your help to get him out of it." As soon as the

words leave her mouth, I shake my head in disagreement. "Please, Blue. I wouldn't ask if it wasn't important," she pleads, wringing her hands.

"Not a chance." I'm sure they can sort out this mess without me. It's not too long since I started trying to accept people, so getting involved in something that might speed it up is not what I'm looking for.

Baby steps, not fucking dinosaur steps.

"You don't even know what I'm going to ask." She straightens her back, watching me with her big hazel eyes.

"It involves me going out?"

"Well. Yes, but—"

"Then no."

Her face drops.

"Ugh, ok, fine. Go ahead and ask."

"Thank you," Olivia says, hope flaring in her eyes. "They broke up a couple of months ago and my parents were really sad when E didn't come home with her, so he panicked and lied about already having another girlfriend."

What? Is he ten? It's not like a new girlfriend is going to replace the other one or make things any better. Lying is a temporary solution. I try to imagine Elias panicking. He seems like such a calm person. A golden retriever.

"Wait. This just keeps getting worse," she laughs, fiddling with the zipper of her hoodie. "When my parents said they wanted to meet her, E said she'd visit this Sunday."

"Oh, shit," I say. Couldn't help it. That's outrageous.

"Yeah, so here's the funny thing: the other day, we were having dinner, and Pa asked E what his girlfriend's name was. Elias looked helpless, which made me panic thinking he would ruin it all." She looks at my left eye, then my right, probably trying to see if I've figured it all out.

I have a vague idea of where this is going. And I don't like it at all.

"And by mistake," she continued, "I said your name."

"What the actual fuck, Olivia?" Back when I was a kid, I used to love being right about things. I wish I wasn't right about this. "Don't your parents know who I am? I mean, you come here every day?"

"Um... They know you go by Blue."

I curse under my breath, not sure how to handle this. Not to mention how to react.

Meeting their parents sounds like my worst nightmare. Pretending to be his girlfriend won't do him any good. They should love him, with or without a partner.

I shake my head, knowing I can't do it.

"Blue, I'm begging you." She grabs my hands, her round eyes pleading. "I promised E I'd get him out of this."

"Then don't make promises you can't keep."

As I walk away, I tell myself I made the right decision, even though her hurt sigh makes my heart ache.

CHAPTER TEN
INDIGO

I SIT AT MY TABLE—THE one closest to the exit—waiting for my date to arrive.

People here are all the same. That might sound weird, considering how distinctive humans are, but this crowd must all be born from the same vagina.

The men are wearing identical tuxedos. The women have tried to stand out with updos and expensive jewelry. Each of them is eating with a ridiculously straight back and using their forks as if they're dining with royalty.

At least the ballroom is pretty. Glossy hardwood, a spiral staircase to the second level, elegant floral arrangements. All the good stuff.

And as much as I'd like to focus on that — it's what I usually do to distract myself from other people's stares — my mind can't stop wandering to Olivia and what she asked me to do.

It's crazy, right?

How could I lie to their family with a straight face? I'm

good at hiding emotions, but that doesn't mean I'd use that skill to play with other people's feelings.

"Indigo," I hear my mother's voice from behind. Goosebumps — not good ones — crawl their way from my back to the tips of my fingers.

I turn in my chair, feigning a smile, only to see her polished face scrutinizing me. Her hair is extra, as usual, with too many white hair clips obscuring her black strands. She has a disgusted look plastered over her features.

Since I moved out, I've gotten over hating her. Now I just don't enjoy being around her or her shitty, unwelcome comments.

"I see you finally took my advice and lost some weight." The fake smile she wears twitches at the edges, her red lipstick looking garish in the light.

"You know I'd never do that," I say. Mom frowns, not understanding. "Take your advice," I explain.

She scoffs, but still manages to do it elegantly. "Act nice. Rowand will be here in a minute."

Mom leaves before I bother to ask her where Dad is. He'll be here, as always, hiding. Ashamed of everything he did.

And he still acts like shit.

I sigh, wishing I wasn't so sober. Mom made it clear how she feels about me drinking at these events. Sometimes, I'd go to the bar and have a shot before they notice me, but tonight I've been too busy wondering if I made the right decision with Elias and Livy.

Hope I did.

It's not long after Mom's set off when the Rowand guy comes into the picture. I see him before he sees me. Large

48

shoulders, hard cheekbones, and no smile on his face. His outfit fits him well, I'll give him that.

He's attractive, the mysterious type you read about in books. There's a dark aura around him and coldness in his eyes that you can see from distance. Well, in my case, from two steps away.

Rowand doesn't say hello, he just sits down, greeting me with a raise of his chin. I hide my shaky hands under the table, picking at my cuticles and I force a smile as a reply.

He has a whiskey glass in his ring-studded hand and lifts it to his lips, staring directly into my eyes. My gaze instantly darts away to the dance floor.

A chuckle reaches my ears and I turn back to him. No anxiety can stop me looking at him now, piercing him with my gaze.

Did he just laugh at me?

"What happened?" he has the nerve to say.

I shrug. "Nothing. Did I say something funny?"

I fake a smile and he shoots me a real one that shows a dimple. For fuck's sake. He's packed with muscles and has great taste in fashion.

Is there anything this guy doesn't have? Oh, yeah. He lacks any sense of humor.

He sits up, fishes a cigarette out of his pocket, and lifts it in the air to indicate that he's going out to smoke.

Rolling my eyes as he turns his back to me and leaves, I pray he'll trip over the stairs on his way out so I can leave this hellish party.

THIS IS the worst part of seeing my parents: taking my contacts out when I get home. They think I have hideous eyes.

Well, fuck you, Jarred and Louise.

I don't care what people think about my eyes. Not that I'm in love with how they look either, but I don't want to spend my life putting my contacts in and taking them out again. I'd rather not bother.

Unfortunately, Rowand didn't smash his head as he was walking down the stairs. After he came back, we ate in silence. He continually checked his watch, like time couldn't pass any slower.

The guy left as he came: with a bob of his head before standing up, and downing his last sip of whiskey.

Oddly, he was the best date my mom has ever chosen.

After washing and drying my face with a towel, I undress and let the gown fall to the bathroom floor. As usual, I lack the energy to clean up after myself. Nothing out of the ordinary.

I put on my favorite hoodie and collapse on the bed, trying to come up with a way to make Olivia's situation better. She's my friend, I guess, so I feel the need to do everything in my power to help her. Hopefully in a way which doesn't require my presence at their home, where they'll bombard me with questions.

And how would I know what to say?

When did you guys meet? How long have you been together? Were you born in Lynbrook? Do we know your parents?

I groan, burying my head in the pillow.

I'm fucked.

CHAPTER ELEVEN
ELIAS

"She's going to do it," Olivia bursts out the back door of Indigo's house, screaming from the top of her lungs.

I stay still, not daring to look back, afraid I must be hearing things.

"Did you hear me?" Livy squeals, her voice buzzing with excitement. "She. Is. Going. To. Do. It." She jumps on my back, wrapping her legs around my torso and her arms around my neck.

"What? How?"

When I turn my gaze to the window, Indigo is standing there, a cute bun in her hair, tight jeans, and a blazer over a short black t-shirt.

There's a crooked smile on her lips, and she shrugs, like she doesn't know what she's doing either.

Resisting the urge to run my hand through my hair, I give her a wave. I smile until my face feels like it might break apart.

Olivia jumps off my back, setting me free from her grasp. I drag my attention from Indigo to my sister, who stares back. She seems pleased about how things turned out, but she's also giving me a look that says *I know something you don't.*

"You like her," she states.

"Well. Yeah. She's just..."

"Different," my sister continues, nodding.

I bob my head in agreement, watching Livy analyze me like an open book. She always reads me, even when I think I'm hiding my feelings. Don't know if that's a good thing or not.

"But not that way," she acknowledges.

"Definitely not that way."

Indigo is a stunning woman. Everything about her is beautiful. It doesn't take a lot to admit I'm attracted to her. She doesn't realize it, but there's something about her that makes you addicted to her presence.

Look at me. I finished my job a couple of days ago and I still come here every day and use her tree as an excuse to see her.

But the last thing on my mind is jumping into another relationship. Technically, it's been a while since me and Ava broke up, but I want to focus on myself a bit. The eight-month practice will help my CV a lot. I'll have to present it to one of the companies my university works with. They help you develop and find a job or, in my case, make your dreams come true.

Olivia's face drops. I pat her head and she scoffs while I gather all the stuff that's laid out in front of the tree.

"Do you still love her?" she says, getting down on her knees to help.

Liv avoids looking directly at me. She just keeps herself busy, biting her lip as she awaits my answer.

We've never talked about serious things like this. Not because I thought she was too young to understand, but I guess we never really had the chance.

She's barely in high school, studying until she graduates. And I was always happy with Ava. At least until she made me realize how much we'd fallen into a routine. Guess it was too late to fight for it. Or maybe she was never really happy and there was no reason left to fight.

"I don't know," I reply sincerely. "I think the only thing I miss is the idea of what we once were."

That's not really love. Is it?

Don't hate her either. Ava gave me a relationship I'll never forget, but she also gave me years of living in the same house, kissing good morning when we woke up, each one of us leaving for work, getting home, kissing goodnight, and occasionally having sex if I wasn't too tired or if she didn't have a headache.

I should've known. Those are the first signs your relationship is slowly ending: coldness, robotically asking how work was, kisses transforming into pecks, and goodbyes that didn't hurt like in the old days.

"Right. Let's go put all of this in the car," says Liv, breaking me from my reverie.

I nod, grabbing a handful of tools and walking towards my car. Olivia stays silent beside me, lost in thought. We put all the stuff in the boot.

"You'll be the one telling her she has only two days to prepare," Liv announces. I sigh. That could make Indigo change her mind.

Won't blame her for it, but I don't have another option, so I might as well try.

"Fair enough," I smile, grab her by the shoulders and kiss her forehead. "We're crazy for doing this, don't you think?"

"Totally," she laughs, and I can't explain how much that sound warms my heart.

We walk back to the house, as I try to come up with ideas for how I should handle this without making it awkward.

Olivia opens the door. Indigo is watching a movie. There's a ton of popcorn spilled on the couch.

My hands go for the pockets of my sweats. Indigo gets up, swallowing a mouthful of popcorn, and pauses the movie.

We stare at each other, unsure how to start this. It's crystal clear that neither of us has been in a situation like this before.

"Um," Olivia walks past us, "I'm going outside with Nova and Kai," she nods, a little smile playing on her lips. "Good luck."

After she leaves, we burst out laughing.

"This is the weirdest thing I had to—"

"I'm sorry for—"

We smile again, a moment of silence passes between us. I gesture to the couch and she nods, her hands shaking slightly as she sits down.

"Why didn't you tell your parents the truth?" she questions, resting her elbow on a pillow and her head in her palm.

Indigo has never really asked me a question before. Well, she's asked a few, but only tiny ones, insignificant. Given the fact she's doing this for me and my sister, I owe her an explanation.

I shrug, feeling ashamed of what I did. "Didn't want to let them down."

She seems pleased with the response, nodding like she understands perfectly.

"My relationship with my ex-girlfriend made them proud," I confess, and her eyebrows raise.

A comfortable silence settles. I feel like we're looking at each other for the very first time. She's gazing at me with heart-stopping eyes while I try to memorize every feature of hers. She has a temptingly curved mouth, exotic cheekbones in a delicate face, and a short straight nose.

"So... is there anything I should know before..." she shifts in her seat, "you know?"

I crack a smile. "You, my *girlfriend*, are a successful businesswoman and you live one hour from Lynbrook."

She laughs and the corners of her eyes wrinkle.

"You went *that* far." She adjusts her position, resting back and swinging both her legs onto the sofa. "How long have we been together?"

"One month."

"How did we meet?"

"Through a mutual friend who introduced us after my breakup. I was reticent at first, but you were fun to be around."

She nods, deep in thought. "So, we were friends initially?"

I nod my head in agreement.

"How old am I?"

I try to remember if I said anything about her age, but I'm pretty sure I didn't.

"Be yourself," I suggest. "Apart from what I've just said, of course."

She blinks, genuinely surprised. "You want me to act like I normally do?"

I nod.

"But why?"

"You won't get lost in lies."

And it's true. Being herself will stop her from over-thinking everything: how she should react, how she should talk, and more. She'll be free to say whatever she pleases and, maybe, who knows, she might even have a good time.

"All right," she nods in agreement. "Is there anything else I should know?"

I clear my throat, trying not to laugh because now is not the time, but I have no other choice but to tell her.

"Oh my God, what is it?" she groans, covering her face with her hands.

"Olivia told them you'd be there on Friday."

She lets out a relieved breath, placing a hand on her chest. Just wait until she hears the rest.

"Okay, yeah. That's not that bad."

"*Mhm*," I murmur, and she raises a brow in question. "Where are you going to sleep since you're not from here?"

Her eyes look like they are going to pop out of her head.

"Fuck me," she growls. "What if we tell them my grandma lives here and I'm going to stay with her?"

I nod. "Yeah, that should work."

"This is fucked up, Elias," she laughs, massaging her forehead with her fingers.

"I know," I laugh. This really is insane.

CHAPTER TWELVE
INDIGO

I'M SHITTING my pants at the thought of meeting his parents, but I have to admit I really enjoyed spending time with him today.

We laughed at the situation we were in, neither of us thinking that a week after we met it would end up like this. I learned so many things about him and he learned a few about me.

He told me plants fascinated him before he could walk and started the process of tree therapy five years ago. Elias is confident that everything will work out for him this year. I don't know much about it, but if there's something I believe in, it's people with big dreams. And Elias is definitely a dreamer.

THE DAYS before the dinner pass in the blink of an eye. Elias and Olivia kept coming over, and our chats continued like normal. No pushing limits or trying to fill the silences.

And now, here we are, all dressed up, ready to leave for a dinner I never thought I'd have.

Elias told me not to go too extra, but not too simple either. I'm wearing a pair of tight blue jeans, a black blouse that skims my body, and some simple make-up.

He should be here any minute, so I walk down the stairs, supporting myself on the banister to prevent myself from falling. My legs are trembling like crazy.

"You look stunning," Enya says, her eyes shining with pride.

She laughed when I told her our plans, but she's pleased I'm getting out of my comfort zone.

When I reach the bottom of the stairs, I stop for a moment to steady my breath. Her warm palm rests on my cheek, sending a wave of peacefulness through me. Sighing, I turn around, ready to run back into my room.

My safe place.

Enya grabs my arm, reading my thoughts. "Stop it," she says. She hugs me, playing with the strands of my hair, her chin resting on my shoulder. "Be yourself."

"This is pointless, Enya." There'll come a time when he must tell the truth. "What if they figure it out?" I take a step back, watching her face. "Oh my God, that would be so weird."

It's safe to say I'm freaking out. For the past two days, I felt excited about this dinner, but the more I think about it, the more I realize how stupid it was for me to be excited to lie to some innocent souls.

Enya shushes me. "They won't, and even if they do, you were just being a great friend."

I shake my head, cracking a laugh. How could this be a

gesture from a great friend?

"I have to agree that I'm not okay with his way of handling things, but why don't you take this as a day in which you're destined to be the woman you want to be?"

I take what she says into consideration. A day free of judgment. A day dedicated to the confident woman I want to be. What do they say? *Practice is key. Fake it 'til you make it.*

"No overthinking."

I smile at that. "No overthinking."

"That's my girl." She takes me into her arms again just as I hear a honk outside.

I breathe a sigh of relief as we break apart. "Okay." Inhale. "Let's do this." Exhale.

"Love you," Enya says as I'm walking towards the door.

"Right back at you."

"Have fun."

I nod and I leave, gathering myself on the front porch. I'm Indigo Hayes, a confident woman with her life all sorted out, and a boyfriend who is taking her to meet his parents.

When Elias sees me approach, he starts the engine. I'm surprised to see him looking agitated. He looks like he might break into a sweat at any second and his palms are gripping the steering wheel, slowly moving back and forth around it.

As I'm rounding the car, he keeps checking himself in the mirror. Like that will ease what he's feeling right now.

I get in and eye him curiously.

"What are you smiling at?" he says.

I didn't even realize I was smiling. I guess seeing him

flustered has amused me.

"It's going to be okay," I say, although I don't know how much it'll help. I'm not used to reassuring people.

He laughs, the green in his eyes sparkles and I notice dimples in his cheeks that I swear weren't there before. That or I didn't pay enough attention.

"I thought you might not come."

"Almost," I admit.

He puts the car in reverse and looks back. A movement that brings his sharp jawline to light. My gaze flicks away, settling on the black stilettos I chose to match my bag.

Elias drives us away and a comfortable silence settles between us. He adjusts the stereo, making the music a little louder.

Dean Lewis. I'd recognize him anywhere and it seems Elias does too, by the way his fingers drum on the steering wheel to the rhythm of *Half a Man*.

We drive past a ton of beautiful houses, the mall, my favorite flower shop, and we're back in the suburbs before he speaks again.

"Thank you." He steals a glance at me.

"Thank me after we're done with this."

"All right," Elias agrees, a slight smile on his face as we park in front of a modest house.

It looks like the perfect place to spend a vacation. Calm. Warm. Inviting. Almost like my house, but this one seems ideal for a crowded dinner, compared to the emptiness of mine.

"You ready?" he asks, looking genuinely interested in how I feel.

"Yeah. Let's do this."

CHAPTER THIRTEEN
ELIAS

I CAN'T EXPLAIN how stressed I was in those twenty seconds it took Indigo to get out of her house. My mind was running through all the worst-case scenarios that could've happened if I went home without her.

But here we are. Me, opening the door for her, and she, looking oddly relaxed. She's never really relaxed. Not since I met her, anyway.

Her brown eye contacts make me sad. I don't think she should hide her eyes. They are beyond beautiful. They make Indigo, Indigo. Indigo wouldn't be Indigo without her different colored eyes, but who I am to tell her what to do?

I give her a reassuring smile before she steps into the house. My parents are already there, waiting for us.

Mom looks like she might cry. This is why I lied: she loves to see her children happy, and if she wants anything more than a dog (my dad said he won't get one, but he'll give in one day), it's for her kids to have a family of their own.

"We're so happy you came," my dad says, going for a hug. Indigo raises her palm for a handshake, but dad bats it away and gives her a tight squeeze.

She doesn't look uncomfortable. To my surprise, she closes her eyes, a smile playing on her lips.

"Oh, honey! You're gorgeous." Mom shoves Dad aside for a hug of her own.

She whispers something in Indigo's ear, and Indigo lets out a laugh and her cheeks go pink.

"I'm Lorelai and this is Tom," says Mom after she lets Indigo go.

Indigo nods. "Thank you for having me," my *girlfriend* says, while my parents beam at her.

I clear my throat and put my hand on the small of her back, guiding her to the dining table. She stiffens under my touch, but doesn't utter a word of complaint. And I tell myself that's what couples are supposed to do. That, and because I *want* to touch her.

Indigo and I laugh as my parents mutter something behind our backs. I drag a chair from under the table and she lowers herself onto it.

Olivia is already seated, too distracted to notice us with whatever she's doing on her phone. When she sees us sit down, her nose raises from the device.

"Hi." Liv jumps off her seat, throwing her arms around Indigo. We're a family that loves hugs.

Come to think of it, I've never hugged Indigo before, but I guess it's not been the right time. Trust me when I say that when you see the look in her eyes, hugging is the last thing you'd think of.

"Hi," Indigo says, hugging Olivia back.

I can tell by the way Indigo is playing with the hem of her shirt as she sits down that she's starting to feel nervous. Maybe that's why I put my hand on her leg, squeezing it a little to comfort her.

Her breath hitches for a second, but when my mother speaks again, her body relaxes. My mother has a talent for making people feel comfortable.

"We're really happy you're here, Indigo."

She nods, a shy smile forming on her lips.

"So," Dad claps his hands together, "who wants to eat?"

Olivia and I raise our forks in the air, a thing we've done since we were little. Indigo watches us curiously, and I don't know what pushes me to do it, but I put my hand on hers and grab the fork for her. She smiles as she raises it with us and Dad smiles back.

"When do you have to get back?" Mom asks, taking the seat opposite Indigo.

"Not until they need me back," she says. I can't believe how smoothly she answered. "And they rarely last a day without me," she laughs, which makes my mom laugh too.

"I was thinking we could watch a movie tonight," Olivia suggests, getting our attention.

Mom nods and smiles broadly, looking at both of us for a response. This is what I love about her. Obama could come to her house and she'd still make everything simple. She doesn't try to impress anyone.

I gaze at Indigo to see what she thinks. Her eyes sparkle like a child's. I nod my head in agreement as a reply for the both of us.

The dinner passes quickly, and my parents come to learn a lot about Indigo. And so do I. There was one moment she tensed, when Dad asked about her parents and she said they'd passed away. I truly felt like the world had slipped from under my feet.

And my hand went to hers again. I squeezed her palm, moving my thumb across her skin. Thought it might help her. Hope that it did.

Now we're all on the couch, popcorn everywhere, and laughing until our tummies hurt. Mostly because Mom made us eat pork, salad, *and* chocolate cake.

We're watching *Dumb and Dumber*, a movie my parents always put on for a good laugh. Whenever they fight, whenever they have a bad day, whenever they feel alone.

Indigo laughs until tears fill her eyes. I've never seen this part of her and it's addictive. She looks up at me, straight into my eyes. We're so close our lips are almost touching. My heart races in my chest as her tongue flicks over her bottom lip. I know that this isn't an invitation, more like an automatic thing, but it takes my breath away.

This is a physical reaction, I tell myself. I won't let it ruin this thing that's going on between us.

So instead of kissing her lips, I lean down and tenderly kiss her forehead.

CHAPTER FOURTEEN
INDIGO

"I THINK it's time for me to go," I say as I get up from the couch.

Lorelai looks a bit crestfallen, as Elias's dad gazes up at me with curious eyes.

"Is everything alright?"

I scratch the back of my head, not ready to leave, but not willing to stay the night either. They're fun and easy to be with, but it's getting late, and I'd like to sleep in the comfort of my own bed.

"My grandma lives here and I promised her I'd stay tonight." I let the lie slip out of my mouth and instantly regretted it.

Both of them nod in understanding with a little smile that doesn't quite reach their eyes. They did nothing but try to make me feel at home. And I did. It makes me feel better than my home ever has.

"Oh," Lorelai says, "I prepared Elias's old room for you guys."

"Maybe Indigo could stay over tomorrow night?"

Elias's dad asks.

I move my gaze from them to Elias, waiting for a way out of this.

"If your grandmother is fine with that, of course," Tom adds, and I can see where Olivia gets her eyes from. Those warm eyes you can't refuse.

It would be good to take a step back, run out of here. But I can't.

I sigh and nod and try to give my best smile. Although I don't completely hate the idea of coming back — and that scares the shit out of me — I don't want to stay the night either. No one's bed is better than mine, but I can't see a way out of coming back tomorrow.

Lorelai squeals, throwing her arms around me. I hear Olivia in the back whispering a loud *yes*, which lowers my stress levels enough to make me laugh. The last time I felt this comfortable in someone's presence was at the party where I had my fake, paid-for date.

This is different, though. This is real. They're not paid to like me. They're not pretending.

"Great." Lorelai releases me from the hug, her palms on my shoulders, and watches me with a big grin on her face.

Can't believe they're fifty. They look gorgeous for their age, their jokes are on point, and Lorelai's cooking is incredible. Oh my god, she made the best meal I've had in ages.

It's surreal to feel so wanted by people I've just met. A night with them is the opposite of a dinner with my family.

Sensing I'm getting lost in thoughts, I shake my head and smile down at her. She's a little woman, a bit like a classic mom you see in movies. When she smiles, wrinkles surround her gentle eyes, and her brown curly hair frames her face beautifully.

Tom and Elias are the same person. Tall, broad-chested, large shoulders, sharp jaw, and green eyes that look like they see through you. Actually, they all have eyes like that.

"Why don't you take Indigo home and I'll clean the dishes?" Lorelai suggests when Elias starts to clear the table.

He puts the plates down, comes behind me, and places his hand on the small of my back. I resist the urge to wiggle free and instead I lean into his touch to make everything between us seem more real.

"Thank you for having me," I say. I hear Elias's breath hitch behind me, making me realize that maybe I'm leaning too close to his hips. "It was amazing meeting you," I continue, straightening my back.

Olivia, Tom and Lorelai are beaming at us. Can't believe they convinced me to stay over tomorrow night. Their power to dominate is unbelievable. Olivia and Elias's parents could ask me to do anything with those big eyes and I'd do it.

"Drive safely!" Lorelai calls as we step out of the house.

My chest tightens as I turn around and see the three of them waving at me. They make such a happy family picture and I tell myself that even if it was only one night, they made it worth it. I wave back.

Elias opens the car door, smiling at me. I get in and so does he. He starts the engine and his family is still there, looking like they could wave for hours.

"Are you okay?" he asks as we drive down the street.

"Mhm."

"I'm sorry," he says.

Not really knowing what for, I frown at him.

"For touching you. That was inappropriate."

I smile at that, covering it with my hand as I lean my elbow on the door.

"What's funny?" I can hear the amusement in his voice.

"You really are respectful."

"Well," he shrugs, "I was raised that way, so I guess you should thank my parents for that. But I'm serious," he continues, stealing a glance at me with earnest eyes, "I'm sorry."

I smirk at him. "Yeah. I know."

He mirrors my smile. "Just say the word and I'll never do it again."

"That was the plan, Elias. Don't feel guilty because I knew what I was getting myself into."

He nods, focusing on the road. "Did you have fun?"

I don't respond at first. I look out the window, remembering the image of his family all smiling and waving at me. As he parks outside my house, I simply say, "Yeah."

It feels hard to admit. Maybe that's why I say it at the last moment, so there's no chance of me bursting into tears in front of him.

As I open the gate, I feel Elias's gaze on my back.

"See you tomorrow?" he says through the car window.

I turn around and nod, then dash into the house. Only after I get in and hear his car drive away do I allow myself to cry.

Throwing off my shoes and bag, I crawl up the stairs, tears streaming down my face.

The bedroom door opens with a thud and I throw

myself onto the bed. I reach out to the bedside, grab my sleeping pills and swallow them without water.

My chest feels like an explosion of feelings. My throat has a harsh lump in it, which doesn't ease until I let out a loud sob. I curl into a ball and cry myself to sleep.

CHAPTER FIFTEEN
INDIGO

THIS MORNING WAS BAD. Enya coaxed me out of bed and forced me to take a shower.

All I wanted to do was spend the day in the safety of my room. Now I'm looking at myself in the mirror, seeing a whole different person than the one buried deep inside me. The girl in the reflection seems calculated. Powerful. Confident. I can't explain how it feels to want to be like her. It doesn't make sense, but she's everything I'm not.

Sighing, I put my contacts in.

Elias is waiting for me outside, so I grab everything I need and walk downstairs. I yell *goodbye* to Enya and dash out the door. I want to leave as fast as possible before I change my mind. But there's no way out of this. So instead of running back inside, I swallow my thoughts and walk towards Elias's car. He opens the door for me from the inside, a small smile playing on his lips.

Everything unfolds like yesterday. We say hi, listen to some music, drive past some of my favorite places, and stop in front of their beautiful house.

I get out of the car before he has a chance to say anything. Elias makes me feel like he knows me inside out. It prickles under my skin. The kind of itch you just can't scratch.

He threw me a couple of glances on our way here. It's clear he suspects something is wrong. It won't be long until he asks questions. Why not postpone it as long as possible?

I stop in front of their door, shaking as the wind sneaks under my clothes. I clasp my hands together to stop myself from picking at my cuticles.

"Don't bother to knock," he says, and I turn to face him.

His gaze travels from my stilettos, all the way up my dark lace leggings, to my tight white top and soft coat, finally reaching my face.

I fidget, feeling my body burn where his glance had wandered.

He threads his fingers between mine, scrutinizing my reaction. "Is this okay?"

I look down at our tangled hands and nod. We enter the house and the smiles of his family make my heart soar. Lorelai rushes forward and hugs me.

"I don't want to be nosy," she starts, and I laugh because it reminds me so much of Olivia, "but you're staying for the night, right?" An expectant smile forms on her lips.

"Yes, of course. As promised," I say, before I'm hugged by the other two members of the family.

"Me and Olivia were making cupcakes. Why don't you join us?" Lorelai says.

I'm no good in the kitchen. Apart from one little thing

my grandma taught me when I was eight, I'm a lost cause with cooking. I could make their job ten times harder.

"Go," Elias encourages me and kisses my forehead.

I nod. Barely keeping my feelings inside, I follow the Madden girls as the boys start the PlayStation in the living room. Lorelai opens the door, revealing a spacious kitchen, with a counter in the middle and lots of cupboards and drawers.

"So," Lorelai says.

"Here we go." Olivia rolls her eyes, making me chuckle.

"Oh, shut up, Olivia," Lorelai smiles, elbowing her daughter. "Elias never tells me anything."

She turns her back to me to decorate the cupcakes and Olivia hops up on the table. Her mom throws her a dissatisfied look, but she doesn't say anything.

"How did you guys meet?"

And that's the first question of many. Fortunately, I have an answer for all of them and Lorelai seems happy. Our *relationship* must seem like a love story from their point of view. And that's how I'm presenting it to her.

I feel sad that there will come a time when she'll find out the truth. I guess it's good that I won't be here when it happens.

The day passes quickly after we finish decorating the cupcakes. I even learn how to play Mortal Kombat. I lost the first three matches and I won the fourth. I think Elias let me beat him. Mortal Kombat is not my cup of tea.

As the fun fades away, Elias and I get closer to being left alone. We say goodnight to the others, I grab my overnight bag from the hallway and Elias guides me to a room upstairs. He opens the door and flicks the lights on.

I'm surprised to see his childhood bedroom looks like this. It's not childish at all. His bed is centered, leaving space for a vast wardrobe and a couple of tables that are mostly covered in plants. It looks aesthetically pleasing.

Clean and white with a bit of green.

He clears his throat and I realize I'm standing in his way. I step aside. As soon as he enters the room, he grabs a pillow and a blanket from the closet and puts them on the floor beside the bed.

I don't know how to react to that or what to make of it, so I just gesture with my thumb that I'm going to the bathroom to change. He nods, continuing to arrange his improvised bed.

I remove my makeup and lenses, strip off my clothes, take my pills, and put on my Winnie the Pooh pajamas. In the mirror, I see a completely broken girl. She looks so tired.

Shaking everything off with a *fuck it* to my reflection, I open the bathroom door. Elias is already on the floor, tucked under the blanket, his arms below his head, gazing at the ceiling.

"Hi," he says, without looking at me.

"Hi."

I sit on the enormous bed and wrap myself in the cover.

"I think this is big enough for both of us if you want to sleep here," I suggest. The floor looks uncomfortable and the bed is huge.

"Nah. I'm good. I want you to sleep comfortably."

I open my mouth to say something, but change my mind. It seems like all my words are getting caught in my throat, blocking anything from getting out.

"It's the least I can do," Elias whispers, and he reaches behind him to switch off the light.

The sadness in his voice can't be described. It pierces my chest.

"It's going to be okay," I mutter, even though it most likely won't be.

"Did I take it too far?"

"Yeah," I reply honestly.

I hear him shift before he speaks. "Did you have fun today?"

I move closer to the edge of the bed, looking down at him. "Yeah."

I can't see his face in the dark, but I imagine he is smiling.

"You did a pretty good job beating me at Mortal Kombat. No one in this house has done it yet."

"Oh, shut up," I laugh, and it seems far away. "You're a bad liar."

"What do you want me to say? That you're terrible?"

"If I am, then yes. Always tell me the truth."

"I've seen worse, but you are *really* bad. Like really, *really* bad."

"So, you did let me win." I raise a brow, although he can't see me in the darkness.

He sighs. "I'm going to have a chat with Olivia."

I laugh at that. "She didn't tell me anything, but you just confirmed it."

"I wanted you to like it. You have to win at least once to like something, right?"

I shrug. "I don't know, but it seems like it worked."

My head falls on the pillow with a soft thud. I don't

know about him, but even with the urge to cry my eyes out, a smile forms on my lips.

"Have a great night's sleep, Indigo," Elias says after the silence settles.

"You too, Elias."

CHAPTER SIXTEEN

ELIAS

Although I don't usually listen in on people's private conversations, it's pretty difficult for me to avoid hearing Indigo's chat, given the fact that I'm in the bathroom. She's talking on the phone with her mom.

Her. Mom.

Why would she tell us her family is dead? That's not a thing to joke about. Talk about lying. No matter how hard I try to find an explanation or to understand her motives, it doesn't make any sense.

The rational part of me thinks that if she didn't want me to know, she wouldn't be speaking with her in the same room as I am, and she'd definitely not call her *Mom*

"I won't bring a date because I'm not coming."

After that, the silence settles and I take it as my cue to get out of the bathroom. I'd been standing in there for over ten minutes so she could finish her call.

I open the door and see her sitting on the edge of the bed, elbows on her knees, hands in her hair. After putting my night clothes in the wardrobe, I sit down next to her, a sigh escaping my lips.

We're sitting close, both of us staring absently around the room rather than at each other.

"Why lie about your mom?" I say.

"Because I'm pretty sure your parents would know mine since they live in town."

I turn my head to look at her. "Do I know them?"

She nods. "Louise and Jarred Hayes." Indigo looks sad at the mention of their name. Her shoulders drop.

"Shit."

They're sort of famous here. Her parents live in a wealthy neighborhood close to hers, and they're well known for the charity parties they host at least once a week. People's opinions about them are divided: the ones that praise them and the ones that think they're scamming everyone.

Don't know which category I'm in.

I nod in understanding. "You could've said something else, though."

"Nah. I wanted to say that," Indigo laughs, smiling awkwardly as a strand of hair falls over her eyes.

I don't know what to take from it. I don't push it any further. "No lying from now on, yeah?" I raise my pinky finger for her to take.

She looks at it from the corner of the eyes, her smirk not leaving her face. "Are we really going to pinky swear?" Indigo looks from my finger to my face.

"It's called sealing a promise," I joke. "But yeah, why not? I want to know that you're in."

She nods, tangling her finger with mine.

"Now, say 'I won't lie to you again'."

Indigo laughs, brushing the hair off her face. I seem to make her laugh a lot these days, and I love how good she looks wearing a smile that's there because of me.

"Just kidding," I shake both of our fingers, "but I would appreciate it if there were no more lies between us from now on."

As she nods in agreement, we break apart.

"And what would you need a date for?" I ask, playfully jostling her with my shoulder.

Indigo shifts in her place and clears her throat, but doesn't respond. I leave it that way, because I don't want her to ever feel pressured to explain something. Indigo has her own pace, like every other person. My job as a friend is to respect it. Not to speed it up.

However, she surprises me a few moments later.

"I'm sure you know about the charity parties," she starts, and I nod. "My mom always pays someone to be my date because of how obsessed she is with finding me a partner."

"What? I would do it for free."

And it's true. No one would need to give me something in return to go out with her. Indigo has a wide range of qualities, including intelligence, charm, humor, and breathtaking beauty.

What kind of person would pay someone to be with their daughter? Wouldn't she want something genuine for her? Forced things rarely work.

She gives a crooked smile, "Yeah, sure."

"I can be your date if that's what you need," I offer, knowing I must pay her back somehow.

Indigo shakes her head. "It wouldn't work."

I frown because, to me, this sounds like it'll solve all our problems. "Why?"

She raises her brows like she's trying to figure me out, but there's nothing to hide. I'm as serious as someone can be.

"That means you'd need to be there every week."

I think for a little. She's right about that. However, an arrangement could help us both avoid unwanted events: me telling my parents that I lied, and Indigo going to parties with random dates.

"Are you looking for a serious relationship at the moment?" I ask.

She grimaces. "Definitely not."

"Good. Me neither." I shift, placing my leg under me. "I'll be your date whenever you need me and you'll be my fake girlfriend," I suggest and she stiffens. "Since neither of us is looking for a relationship, we could do this to get rid of the pressure from our parents."

She looks from one of my eyes to the other, and I do the same. I can see the wheels turning in her head.

"You'll need to spend *hours* clothes shopping," she says.

I nod, although shopping is not my favorite hobby.

"You'll need to accompany me every week for a few hours, shaking hands with people you don't know. And my parents are not as sweet as yours."

A shiver runs down my spine at the thought, but I ignore it. "Okay."

She raises her brows, eyes big. "I like your parents."

"They like you too."

"And I don't want to lie to them."

"Then don't. Be yourself. You only need to lie about us being together," I say, the words feeling salty on my tongue.

If there's one thing I hate, it's lying to the people I love. There's no way back from this, though.

"How can I be myself if you presented me as the girl who has her own freaking company?" She puts her hands on her hips.

I shrug. "What do you do for a living?"

"My family is rich, remember? I literally walk dogs and nothing else."

"Same thing," I laugh. She laughs. And I can't explain how good this feels. It feels like her laugh is a precious win.

"Deal." Indigo throws herself on the bed, looks up at the ceiling and I do the same.

"We should stop as soon as there's someone else."

She nods, brooding over it.

We sit in comfortable silence until there's a knock on the door. Neither of us has time to sit up before my mom comes in with a hand over her eyes, gaps between the fingers so she can peek through.

Nosy woman.

It's good we woke up earlier to gather the improvised bed and for Indigo to put in her lenses.

"Are you guys dressed?"

I laugh and sit up, "Yes, Ma."

Mom uncovers her eyes, smiling at both of us.

"Change, we are going to play darts," she smiles at both of us. "Or don't. Love your pajamas." Mom winks at Indigo, who turns pink and looks down at her Winnie outfit.

I can tell Mom is hurt by me and Ava breaking up, but

it's crystal clear she wants everything to go back to normal. When Ava came over, we always used to go play darts. Although it was a tradition before I could even walk, she became a part of it.

I laugh and push my mom out of the room, letting her know we'll be down soon. When I turn around, Indigo's peering down at her pajamas.

"Did your mom just make fun of me?"

CHAPTER SEVENTEEN
ELIAS

DAD HAS ALWAYS BEEN the best at darts. That's why it's no surprise he's won three times already. What I'm surprised about is Indigo being right behind him. There's a tight score between them.

"Let her win," Mom whispers into Dad's ear.

My dad turns to look at her, mouthing a proud *never*. It seems that Indigo noticed, since she eyes them, laughing. Dad turns to her and shrugs like he owns the game.

"Don't worry, I'd rather win because I deserve it," says Indigo.

"*Mmhmm*," Dad nods. "Then get ready to lose again."

"Hey," Olivia pouts, "I'm right there with you."

Mom and I always fight for the last place. Even though we've played this game for years, we're still incredibly bad at it.

"Your turn, Mom," I remind her, with a tap on her shoulder.

"Oh," she puts her coffee down, "right."

She straightens her back, the three arrows gripped in her

tiny hand. Mom closes one eye, as if that would ever help, and aims for the board, missing it by a mile. Dad tries to explain it to her for the hundredth time, so I take it as my cue to go check on Indigo.

"Are you having fun?" I ask her.

She looks up at me from where she's sitting, eyes sparkling. I don't need a response from her. The eyes always tell the whole story.

"Is it so hard for you to let me win *once*?" Livy asks, drained from the games we've already played.

Dad laughs, placing his arm on her shoulders. He drags her close and kisses her blonde hair.

"Where would all the fun be?" he laughs, looking down at her. "Won't it feel better when you win because you worked hard for it?

"No." She raises her brows at him. "A win is always a win, no matter what."

We all laugh at that because she's kind of right. That's how things work these days. People only want the win, no matter what they have to do to get it.

We play a little more, then all start yelling when Indigo wins. I don't know what makes me do it, but when I see her excited, her arms clearly open for a hug, I go all in. I grab her middle, raise her in the air, and spin around.

Her winning the game means Dad will finally stop praising himself. It also means she's not as bad at everything as she is at Mortal Kombat.

I stop whirling her around, but my hands stay on her waist. Dark alluring eyes gaze up at me, blinking several times before she steps back. The all-consuming eye contact stops as she twirls a strand of hair behind her ear. That's always a warning sign for her.

"I guess you're too old, Tom," Mom laughs, patting Dad on the back.

"Nah. It was pure luck." He smiles down at Indigo, giving her a high five. "Not going to happen again." Father points at her and she cracks a laugh.

"Yeah, only because Dad will train to get back at you," Olivia says.

He shushes her, making those big eyes that mean *don't you dare say anything else*.

"WHAT?" Indigo mutters into her phone, shoulders tensing. We just got home after playing darts when her cell rang. "How?" Indigo's heavy lashes fly up in shock.

She stops pacing my room and her body stiffens. She drops the phone from her ear.

I want to help, but there's nothing I can do, especially because I don't know what's happening.

Indigo quickly straightens up, puts her phone in the back pocket of her jeans and rushes toward the bathroom. I sit up from the bed to stop her.

"What happened?" I say.

She sighs, her alarmed breath calming for a short moment. "They're taking Mushroom down."

I frown. Who in the world would do that? It's her property. "I'll go with you."

She seems surprised by my offer. Her bottom lip quivers as her shaky hands grab a fistful of her hair. "What? No."

"Yes. Let's go."

She doesn't move, her eyes look blank. I grab her by the hand and open the door. Olivia is standing there, blinking. If I hadn't been used to her nosy attitude, this would've scared me.

The cheeky smile that was on her face disappears when she sees our expressions.

Livy was never the one to be excited about making new friends. That's exactly why I think Indigo and the tree mean so much to her. Mushroom has become a project for me, but seeing the way my sister interacts with him makes me care about him more.

I want to convince people that plants can get better if you talk to them, and, in return, they can make you better. They're therapeutic.

"What?" Olivia asks.

I give Indigo a little push in the back with my finger and she starts walking towards the stairs. Grabbing Liv, we follow the black-haired girl.

"They want to cut the tree," I whisper. "I don't know much else yet."

She nods, looking up at me as we walk. "Can I come?"

"Sure." I take her nose between my fingers, and she bats my hand away with a sad smile.

Mom is in the lounge when we get down. She sits up from the couch and pauses her movie.

"Where are you guys going?"

I see Indigo trying to form a response in her head. Her lips open and close a few times before I decide to speak for her.

"Her grandmother would like to see us."

She smiles warmly at that, nodding her head in agreement.

"One moment." Mom raises a finger and goes into the kitchen. "Are you guys staying for the night?" she yells, pots clanging.

I look at Indigo, seeing how disconnected she is, and I don't know if she'll accept our help, but whatever the outcome, we have to be there for her. That's what friends do.

"Yes," I say. Olivia looks up at me, but Indigo still doesn't say a word. "If you don't mind," I add as Mom enters the room with a tub full of sweets.

"Have fun and give these to her," Mom smiles, and Indigo gives the tiniest smile back.

We go to the door and say our goodbyes. On the way to Indigo's house, all I can think about is how to make it better.

CHAPTER EIGHTEEN
INDIGO

I'M ALREADY LEAPING from the car before it stops and running into the backyard. Elias and Olivia shout after me, but their voices seem distant. The thought of getting there too late is all-consuming.

I hear Enya before I see her. "Sir, just wait!"

I round the corner of the house and I'm nearly knocked down by the image before me. A guy with a yellow hardhat has his hands on his hips. He turns to look my way as the bulldozer behind him starts to move.

Knowing that Liv and Elias are here gives me the strength I need to walk toward my nightmare.

I take a deep breath, trying to stop my hands from shaking, knowing that now is not the time to lose my voice.

"Can we talk?" I say as I get closer to Enya and the man.

"I already spoke with the lady here," he says, motioning to Enya. "There's nothing more to talk about."

"You're on private property. You're obligated to do whatever the owner says," Elias intervenes. I try to hide my surprise at the way he stands up for me.

"I am not." The guy takes a step back and I take one forward, feeling the two behind me do the same. "Now let us do our job," he says.

My blood boils in my veins and I feel like hitting him. No matter how hard I clench my fists, those violent thoughts don't stop.

Tears fill my eyes and I suddenly feel like I'm eight years old again. Everything I love somehow gets lost or taken from me. It's not fair. Why can't it stay? It's mine. My grandma's. The tree is the only thing I have left of my childhood. Nothing else. Just memories that will slowly fade and die.

The workman laughs, a smug look on his face that makes me want to punch it. I've never been violent in my whole life. I might take my chance today, though.

"Miss," he takes a step closer to me and I feel Elias at my back, "I'm afraid that this is not your property." The guy throws an unimpressed look at Elias, probably letting him know he's not intimidated by him.

He takes a map out of his jeans pocket, opens it, and shows it to me. The drawing proves that I only have the house and the garden. The stretch of ground beyond the garden, including Mushroom, isn't mine.

"Clear enough?" he sneers.

"Be respectful, eh?" Elias says. "You can't just take away half her yard without answering some questions."

"My job is to take this tree down and leave."

Elias curses under his breath. I think this is the first time I've seen him pissed. The man turns to leave, but I try one more time.

"I'll buy it."

It seems like the only option right now. I have a ton of money, so that won't be a problem. I'll pay any amount.

"You can't. I'm afraid that this is no longer city property. A developer bought it." He backs away. Just like that. Crushing me under his foot.

"There's no way I could buy it?"

"No. They're planning to build here." The guy says with his back to us, while he signs to the man in the bulldozer to cut Mushroom's trunk.

And we just stay there. Watching Mushroom get destroyed, along with my most beautiful childhood memories. None of us move.

I feel like the tree is taking bits of each of us with him. We're all connected in different ways and we all suffer in silence.

The tree brought peace to me when I was little and comfort when I grew up. He brought Olivia to me, and then Elias.

Even though I don't know where my friendship with Elias is going, he's here right now. They are here. And I can't remember the last time someone was there for me.

Olivia cries and comes to hug me. I just stand there, with no strength to react. No tears. Nothing. On my left, I can see a tear sliding down Enya's cheek, and when she senses that I'm watching her, she joins us in the hug.

Elias sniffs and then I feel his comforting touch on my shoulder. I want to lean my head on it, but Enya rouses us, bringing me back to reality.

"Let's go," she says.

I nod, and we all turn away. None of us look back as we leave.

"You go in. I'm going to get the sweets from the car," Elias says, but I stop him before I change my mind.

"Can we go to your parents?"

If he's surprised, he doesn't show it. He nods and Olivia squeezes my hand.

"Just let me get Enya the sweets and then we can go," he says.

I nod in agreement and sit down on the porch.

"I like him." Enya says.

I try not to think about a life without the biggest memory keeper I've had. Because that's what he was to me. The reminder of all the beautiful things that happened here with my grandma. And now he's gone. Just like everything else that once made me happy. Were they even real? Or was it all in my imagination?

After that, everything happens in a blur. Enya takes the sweets and we drive to Elias's parents' house in complete silence. They're there to greet us when we arrive.

If they sense there's something wrong, which I'm sure they do, they don't say anything about it. His dad suggests playing Mortal Kombat, which we do, and I somehow manage to beat everyone. His father laughs at Elias about that, and we feel a little lighter, but that space in our hearts is spoiling every smile, every laugh.

Lorelai tries her best to please our tummies with everything she has. We eat almost robotically, and I notice the concerned looks between Tom and Lorelai.

"Let's go to bed," Elias says, putting his hand over my shoulder as the clock approaches midnight.

Olivia sits up. "I'm going too."

We all say good night, each of us going to our rooms.

When we enter Elias's, I crash on the bed, and Elias starts to make his.

I stop him. "Sleep here. You don't have to sleep on the floor."

He pauses, looking concerned.

"We are *adults*. Come on."

Elias nods, stretching on the bed as far away from me as possible. I don't read anything into that, because even though he might not be attracted to me, I know my worth.

It feels weird to have someone next to me, and I guess it's because I've embraced sleeping alone as a therapy in one way or another. My bed is my safe place. The space where I cry, sleep, and relax.

I've always thought sleeping with another person would violate my privacy. And I still do. The only difference now is the events of the last few hours. It's like I'm aware he's beside me, but at the same time, it's the last thing I care about.

We stay like that for a long time, facing the ceiling, fully dressed. I try to hold it back, but a sob rips through my chest. I turn my back to him, afraid he might find it childish, but he stops me.

"Don't." He scans my face, his eyes full of worry.

I nod, although this feels like giving him everything I have. I feel so vulnerable. I'm at his mercy.

"Can I—?" he asks, opening his arms.

I don't reply to that. I just fall into his embrace quietly and let his arms wrap around me. I inhale the scent of summer on his skin. He smells so good.

And, if I think about it, I've never needed a hug as much as I do now.

CHAPTER NINETEEN
ELIAS

I WOKE up earlier and got some things done in town. By the time I got home, Indigo had decided to head back to her place. It took me by surprise, if I'm honest. It was obvious she'd go back to her house at some point, but this didn't seem like the time. At least that's how it felt for me.

Although her request to spend last night here was unexpected, I'd assumed she'd stay for a while. Guess I was wrong about that. Can't blame her either. She probably needs some space after all that happened.

I was going to leave town tomorrow anyway. Something I'm not looking forward to, but it'll happen whether I like it or not.

I offer to drive Indigo home and we park in front of her house and sit in silence.

She didn't deserve this, nor did Olivia. Life isn't fair, but it hurts the most when it fucks with people you care about. And I care about Indigo. Like I care about any other human. Seeing others hurt affects me. It's not something I can control.

"I'm really sorry," I whisper, not knowing what else to say.

"Thank you," she says without looking at me, and starts to get out of the car.

"Wait up."

I get out first, rounding the vehicle so I can open the door for her. She steps out, confused, almost like she's walking on ice, careful with every move she makes.

"Come on," I shake my head and close the door after her, locking the car. I stand behind her and put my hands over her eyes.

"What's happening?"

"Just walk," I encourage her, but she doesn't take any steps forward. "Please."

Indigo sighs and steps away like it's the first time she's walked. "If I fall, you're paying the hospital bill."

I laugh and give her a push when we go past the gate. She growls. I chuckle.

"I'm not going to let you fall, Indigo."

"You know I know where I am, right? I know this place like the back of my hand."

She tries to walk a little more confidently, but I put my foot in front of hers, almost making her trip. I grab her in time, laughing about it. She stops and stomps on my foot as hard as she can, but I hardly feel it.

I give her a gentle push to start walking again, but she refuses to move.

"Where are we now?" I ask her.

"Front garden, left side, close to the front door," she responds, surprising me with how aware she is of her surroundings.

"Alright. Let's keep moving."

She shakes her head like a child, hugging her chest.

"Oh, come on." I try not to laugh.

"Oh my God, you're still laughing," she states, raising her foot to stomp on mine again, but I'm fast enough to move it a few inches back.

"I was just joking around."

"I don't trust you."

For a moment, I think about carrying her in my arms, but I think better of it. She wouldn't like it.

I remove my hands and say, "I can show you from here, anyway. Open your eyes."

"Show me what?" Indigo asks, as I turn her towards the hammock.

At first, she doesn't see it.

When she does, she gazes at it, then at me. At it, then at me.

I shrug. "Go take a look."

"Are you serious?"

Nodding, I place a hand on the small of her back, leading her towards it.

"Are you kidding?" she turns around, checking my face.

"Why would I be kidding?" I genuinely ask, staring into those brown contact lenses of hers. They seem like a shield, hiding her true self. She feels far away when she's wearing them.

We stop, looking at the little tree I planted for her.

"I–," she starts, lowering to her knees and touching it.

"I know it's not the same—"

Indigo interrupts me with a shake of her head. She opens her mouth a few times as if trying to get the words out, but every time she comes up empty. She's looking down at it like it's the most beautiful thing someone has ever done for her. I doubt that.

"You can see it grow and I'll be here to teach you everything about it."

Her hands shake as she places them in the back pockets of her jeans. It wasn't my intention to make her emotional. All I wanted was to make it better. Don't really know why. Don't care either. You don't need a reason to help someone or be good to them.

"If you want me to, of course," I add when she still doesn't say anything.

She nods in agreement, her eyes glistening.

I turn my head and act like I didn't see it. "Well, if you need—"

She cuts me off by throwing her arms around me.

I do the same, inhaling her strong scent as her body heat sends warm waves through me.

She smells nice. Can't really tell what perfume she's wearing. While it won't make you sneeze, it's strong enough to ensure that once you become aware of it, you can't ignore it.

"Thank you," Indigo says, and when she takes a step back, there's no trace of tears.

I don't know how she can do that. My eyes go puffy and my cheeks turn red whenever I cry. She looks like she just stepped out of a magazine.

"Don't thank me too much or I'll get used to it," I laugh. I hate that she still can't make eye contact with me. Am I making her uncomfortable? She seemed to be getting used to me lately. Not sure about now, though. "Did you say you like dogs?" I ask, changing the subject.

Indigo studies my face for a few seconds before nodding.

That's a good thing. I love dogs. I always have. Knowing she's an animal lover makes me feel a bit better about tomorrow. Maybe once I come back, her mood will lighten.

"I'm going out of town tomorrow," I blurt. I don't know why I say it so suddenly. It just slips out of my mouth.

"Oh."

It's my turn to nod. I kick a rock and bury my hands in the pockets of my jeans.

The creak of a door gets our attention.

Enya is standing on the porch. "How do you like it?" she smiles. "I wonder what name we could give this one."

We all burst out laughing, Indigo's mood changing in an instant. I'm pretty sure we all know that Olivia is going to choose it.

CHAPTER TWENTY

ELIAS

Avocado throws himself at me, and I grab him just in time.

"Hi, buddy," I say in a high-pitched voice as he licks my face from top to bottom. "Hi," I repeat, as he wiggles in my arms. I'm trying so hard not to drop him.

He's the biggest and fluffiest Golden Retriever on earth, and he's a sucker for sweet talk.

"Daddy missed you." I tap his nose, and he licks my finger. "Yes, he did."

I step in, close the front door, and put him down. Ava steps out of the bedroom. She's dressed only in a white t-shirt and underwear, and it's such an Ava thing to do. She loves to walk around the house as naked as possible. I loved it too, for a while.

Now it only makes me laugh, knowing how she must spend her time. Especially now she has the entire place to herself.

"Oh, hi. I didn't know you were coming."

I open my mouth to say something, but a shirtless man appears from the bedroom and I just nod. I'm not surprised. There's a big chance she was with other guys before we broke up. Can't blame her either.

"Who's this?" the guy questions, raising a brow at her.

"I'm Elias." As soon as I say my name, his face clears in understanding. "I'm just here to grab Avocado."

Ava's face drops. "You're not taking him." She's fighting me, but not really.

"You can come visit him."

I had Avocado before I met her, and although I know how much she loves him, that doesn't mean she gets to keep him. She's free to see him whenever she wants, but I'm not going to be apart from him any longer.

The guy leaves the room, looking awkward.

"I–", she starts.

"Ava," I warn. I'm not going to back down.

It's weird how I don't feel jealous of the guy. I actually think it's good for her. We didn't work. Things like this just happen, and a high school romance doesn't always lead to marriage. Living in a family like mine, you'd believe it does. You'd believe that loving someone is enough. Well, it's not.

Although my parents have been together since they were fourteen, a love like theirs can be hard to find. Not all of us can marry our first love.

Ava nods and steps towards us, her eyes welling up. She picks up Avocado, hugs him, and kisses his head.

It must be hard for her. It was the same for me. Stubbornness was the one thing keeping me from him. Guess the need to be anywhere but in the same house as her was strong enough to do that, but it would've felt weird to do otherwise after the way we ended things.

"I'm going to miss you," she whispers, inhaling his scent.

Avocado licks her face, and she lets out the little laugh I used to adore. She looks up at me, the dog still in her arms.

"How are you?" she says.

It's the first nice thing she's asked me since we broke up. We were pretty mean to each other and threw a lot of guilt around. It didn't help. If a relationship comes to an end, it's normally the fault of both people.

I shrug, "Pretty good."

She nods, kissing Avocado again. "Have you met anyone?"

My mind flicks to Indigo. "Yes, but not in the way you think." I place my hands in my jeans pockets and she smiles. "What?"

"Then it's definitely that way." I frown, and she shakes her head at me, putting Avocado down. "That's the same thing you said about me."

I try to remember when I said that, but I come up empty. As far as I can recall, I liked Ava since I was fifteen. She kept refusing me until I turned sixteen. Something changed that year. I'm not sure what, though.

"If there wasn't anyone, you would've just said no."

"Then, no."

"If you say so," she shrugs. The guy joins us again, this time with a shirt on.

After that, we chat about mundane things while I pack Avocado's things and some other stuff I left.

I don't know if I should move back to Lynbrook. If I

do, I don't want to live with my parents. I should find my own place. That'd be good for Avocado and me. Silence. A fresh start. I just need to figure out how to do it.

I check if I have everything and put the house key on the table. They lead me to the door, Avocado walking beside me.

"Goodbye, Ava." I smile. "Bye," I say to the guy, so he knows there are no hard feelings.

Avocado and I leave and relief washes over me. I was expecting this to be a lot harder, but I feel like I can finally let go of everything.

I get into the car and Avocado jumps onto my lap. While I pet him, I do something I've never done before: I search for Indigo on social media. An account pops up with a profile picture of her next to the tree, smiling.

I tap on the little icon, surprised to see how many followers she has. Weird. I've never seen her spending time on her phone.

Most of her feed is green. Plants. Nature. Mushroom. There's one that stands out, though. One of her, when she was little with an old lady who I guess was her grandma. She has beautiful, gentle eyes. The woman is hugging Indigo tightly to her chest, grinning. The caption says: 'Fly high, but not too far'.

I wonder if I'm prying too much, but curiosity gets the better of me, so I check her story as well.

The first photo is of her, dressed in a muddy outfit in the garden. The next one shows her entire garden, which is insanely gorgeous, and my heart flutters a little when I notice the tree I planted for her. The last one is just the new tree with a watering can. It's an artistic photo that looks like it came straight from Pinterest.

I smile at that and Avocado barks, making me laugh.

"Let's go, buddy." I pet him and he makes himself comfortable in the passenger seat. "It's time for us to find a new home."

CHAPTER TWENTY ONE
INDIGO

IT'S BEEN EXACTLY a week since I left Elias's house. Now it's finally time to get out of bed, dress up, and spend another night at a party I hate.

I take a shower at the slowest pace ever. Once I'm out, I wrap myself in a towel and leave my hair to air dry.

"Indigo!"

I jump, my breath hitching. Jesus Christ. This woman is going to kill me one day.

"Yes?" I yell back at Enya, trying to calm the rapid beating of my heart.

"He's coming!"

I hear heavy footsteps and instantly freeze. I open my mouth to ask who it is, but I stay quiet when I hear the footsteps outside my bedroom door.

Luckily, I have all my clothes stuffed in my wardrobe. There are still a few things here and there, but at least there's no more evidence of the mess I live in.

"Are you dressed?" A voice I instantly recognize says.

I look down at myself. "Kind of?" I say.

"Are you covered enough?"

"Yeah, I guess."

Elias opens the door. He looks great in jeans and a checked shirt. His broad chest is enhanced by the close-fitting fabric. Elias looks at me, analyzing my body from my toes to the tips of my wet hair. Somehow, he manages to do it respectfully.

"Why didn't you call?" he asks as our eyes lock.

"What do you mean, *why I didn't call*?"

"We talked about me going with you to your parents' parties, remember?"

I close my eyes and wonder how Elias found out about this. When I open them, he's staring at me with a sad look on his face.

"What happened?" he mumbles.

I shrug, turning to face the mirror so I can continue doing my makeup.

"Nothing happened." I try to stay as steady as I can, so I won't ruin my eyeliner. "I just know that these parties won't make you happy, so why torture you?"

I catch him fidgeting from the corner of my eye. He lets out a loud sigh.

I turn abruptly. I'm kind of pissed at him. He could've just stayed home and not bothered me when I'm already in a hurry. "What?" I snap.

"Look, I understand where you're coming from," he takes a step forward, "but I'd really appreciate it if next time you'd ask me if I want to do it or not."

Swallowing the lump in my throat, I nod. He must realize I'm not convinced when I turn back to the mirror.

Elias approaches and gently turns me around by my

shoulders, forcing me to look into his eyes. He's close, but not too close. "I want to go, okay?" he says. He inclines his head, trying to get a better view of my eyes, as if he'll get the answer from them.

"Yeah, sure," I blurt.

"It's not because you helped me. I want you to know that," he says, and I raise a brow. He laughs, and my heart breaks a little. "Sure, that's a factor too, but I want to help you."

I nod. "Well, you can't," I quickly put my foundation on.

"Why?"

"Unless you're a doctor with a whole lot of money." I smile sarcastically at him. "Let me just change."

I don't wait for his reaction. I just start to gather my outfit, taking out every piece of clothing one by one.

"Why can't I just be me?" he asks while I look through my dresses.

"Because," I start and choose a black one, "my mom wanted to couple me with another man tonight, so I said I'm already bringing someone else." I go behind my changing screen so I can put on my underwear and throw the dress over my head. "She had the damn nerve to laugh in my face and then she said I could never find a *proper* man."

I come out from behind the dressing screen. "Zip me up," I say and point over my shoulder.

He does so without saying a word. His fingers graze my skin and I get a shiver up my spine.

"So, I said to my mom, 'You know what, fuck off, Mom. I have this amazing doctor that is richer and smarter than any man you could bring tonight.' And then guess what?" I turn to face him.

He raises his eyebrows in question.

"She fucking said, 'Oh, that's lovely, looking forward to meeting him tonight.'"

He grimaces, and I frown at the weird face he's making.

"Are you constipated? Do you need to use the bathroom or something?"

He bursts out laughing, tears filling his eyes as he tries to cover his laugh.

"What's funny?"

He swallows and sits on the edge of the bed, massaging his temples, no longer looking amused.

"Nothing," he admits. "Nothing. I think it's just tiredness." He rubs his face as if trying to wake himself up.

I sit next to him and sigh. "We are so fucked up."

"Yeah. I thought it was funny how I lied to my parents because I was too scared to tell them about my relationship ending, and then how you lied to your mom because of how she controls your life."

I nod. "It seems like we're both controlled by our parents, but in different ways."

"Yeah."

A moment of silence passes between us. I bite my lip. He bounces his legs. I play with my cuticles.

"Well?" he says. "Do you have an outfit or something?"

CHAPTER TWENTY TWO
ELIAS

"STAY STILL," Indigo demands, buttoning my shirt.

I've never in my life had so many pieces of clothing on me. They feel like they weigh more than I do.

My mouth curves into an unconscious smile as I watch her brows draw together in concentration. Her nose is wrinkling, and her eyes squint. She looks like she changes her mind, unbuttons my jacket, then vest, and tosses them on the bed. She pulls one corner of my black shirt from my pants.

Indigo sticks her tongue in the corner of her mouth while she gets rid of my belt, then shuffles her fingers through my hair. She pats my shoulder before turning me around to look at myself in the mirror.

I look different. Good different. My usual style is pretty plain. Jeans, white t-shirt, and a jacket. Sometimes pants, black t-shirt and a hoodie. I'm not a colorful guy. And she didn't change that, but she somehow made me look better.

Can't say I have the appearance of a doctor, but I do look like a wealthy man that doesn't care about showing how rich he is, keeping everything simple. Honestly, that's something I'd do.

She picks up the jacket she just threw on the bed, the one that matches the gray pants. "Take this with you."

I grab it as she rounds the bed to pick up her purse, stepping over a few books and painting brushes.

When she whirls around to me, she shakes her head. "No, hold it with two fingers only, over your shoulder." She shows me how to do it and it feels unnatural. "And be more confident. You look good." She pats me on the back and walks towards the door.

I linger behind, allowing myself a moment to admire how great she looks in that tight dress that accentuates her slim waist as it flares into rounded hips. It's long, but hugs her legs and has a slit that shows her shiny skin.

"Are you coming?" she asks, turning to look at me.

I nod, thinking the gleaming necklace she's wearing doesn't hold a candle to her natural beauty.

I SUPPOSE I was so focused on helping Indigo that I forgot how many hands I needed to shake tonight. Other types of touch don't bother me, but handshakes do. It's because people never wash their hands. Men, in particular. They pee, zip up their fly, and walk out of the bathroom.

Other than that, I'm actually having a good time. Indigo's presence consumes me, and every time she shifts, my gaze is drawn to her, making me forget what I'm saying to people mid-conversation.

You'd think I'm in love with her by the way we interact,

by how my hand lingers on the small of her back, by how she leans into me without realizing it.

She's charming and if I didn't know any better, I'd say she's enjoying her time here. But I do know better. And I do notice things that others seem to ignore, or they simply don't care to look for. Like now, when her hand is trembling slightly as she sips from her drink.

In front of us is a tall man who introduced himself as Leo Twitcher, a guy who was her date a while ago. Every time he speaks, I can feel her body stiffen under my touch.

"Could you excuse us for a moment?" Leo pins me with his gaze, a gaze that was on Indigo just seconds ago. "We're in the middle of a conversation." He gestures with his hand to Indigo and then himself.

I've never wanted to punch someone more than I want to punch this guy. He has this look on his face that says *I'm full of shit and I love to make a show out of everything*.

Indigo looks pissed, her face turning a dark shade of red.

"I'm sorry, but we have to go," I say. "It was really nice to meet you, Leo." I grab her hand and lead her to the dance floor.

Her eyes widen, but she doesn't complain. I nod, encouraging her to just trust me with this one. She sighs, placing her hands on my shoulders, and I place mine on her back. We're the only ones dancing.

"I don't like to dance," she hisses.

I chuckle, knowing how much I hate it myself. "We can go back to chatting with Leonardo Di Caprio if you want," I joke and she instantly stiffens. "That's what I thought."

"He was the worst," she admits, a disgusted look on her face, "but we can't dance all night to avoid everyone."

I shrug, "Why not?"

"Because these shoes are already slicing my toes open." Indigo stops for a second, shaking one leg and then the other.

"Then take them off."

She looks up at me like I've just said the dumbest thing ever. It's just something my mom loves to do whenever her feet are sore, and she wants to keep dancing. She really is the life of the party.

"No." She straightens her shoulders.

"Why?"

"Because I said so." She looks so sassy when she rolls her eyes.

"Yeah?" I ask, raising my brows.

Indigo looks around her at the sea of people. Some of them ignore us, others smile, and some look at us like we're animals in a zoo. Can't say it's comfortable for me.

"Yes, Elias," she hisses, her gaze still on the surrounding people.

I catch her off guard and lift her into the air, one arm under her shoulders, the other under her knees, and spin her around, while carefully slipping her shoes off with the tips of my fingers. They fall on the floor as her eyes shoot daggers.

Smiling might not be the best thing to do when she's fuming, but I can't help it. She's too absorbed in all this formal shit. Indigo needs to loosen up a little.

I keep swaying us to the rhythm of the music and laugh at her frustrated expression. She looks like she wants to murder me, but at least she'll laugh about it years from now.

She checks her surroundings once again, and I look up myself, noticing all the attention on us. And when I say all of it, I really mean it. People are taking videos. Even the security guy is staring at us.

"Everyone is looking at us thanks to your smart ass," she groans, burying her head in my chest.

"Let them look. Ten percent of them are curious, the rest are envious."

She murmurs something so quiet I can't hear it, but I bet she's swearing, so I just laugh it off and keep dancing.

CHAPTER TWENTY THREE
INDIGO

JUST AS I start to relax into Elias's embrace, a cold tap on my shoulder brings me back to reality. I know who it is without looking. I take a deep breath and keep my gaze locked on Elias.

He slowly nods and gently puts me down.

I still don't look up at my parents as I'm straightening my dress and putting my shoes back on. Elias puts his hand around my waist, squeezing it enough to convince me to face them.

My right hand brushes Elias's and my first reaction is to take it away, but then I remember where we are. So I grab it. He breathes in deeply and smiles at my parents.

"Mom," I finally say, looking at her tacky outfit, "Dad." I nod my head towards him and he nods back, quickly moving his gaze from me to the rest of the room, sipping from his martini.

"I see you took my advice." She raises her chin and points at my dress. No *hello*. No *how are you?* Straight to the point, like usual. "Aside from your arm fat, you look surprisingly good tonight." She says it with a look on her face that's eerily like how I look after eating pickles. And I detest pickles. The smell alone makes me want to throw up.

Elias grunts quietly. His chest puffs and I'm surprised to see him taking my mom's hand and kissing it.

He looks like he ate pickles too. I almost snort at that but keep my mouth shut when Mom raises her eyebrows, giving me a wink when Elias has his head bent to her hand.

Elias shakes hands with dad, while they exchange names and pleasantries.

"So nice to meet you," he politely says.

Dad gets back to his game of *looking at everyone but my daughter* and then Mom starts to question Elias.

"So, Elias, tell me, what's it like to be a doctor?"

Her eyes sparkle with challenge, and I feel him stiffening next to me.

"Not that great, actually."

Mom's eyebrows shoot up in surprise. She's a big fan of drama.

"It's not that I don't love my job, but it can be really tough when you lose someone."

He's not entirely lying. Plants are his patients after all. He deals with loss, too, so that's probably helping to prevent my mom from sniffing out the lie.

She nods her head in agreement, keeping her mouth shut. She plays with her necklace and bites her bottom lip. Relief washes over me when I realize she won't continue this line of questioning.

"Well," she starts, grabbing my father's arm, a sign they'll leave, "we're expecting to see you next weekend?"

Elias opens his mouth to respond, but she quickly speaks before he does. "Unless you're busy saving lives, of course."

I cringe at her voice, so full of disbelief and defiance. I guess she can't be silent for more than two seconds. Or respectful.

"Of course," he smiles and I can hear his false tone, even if my mom doesn't trace it.

My parents turn to leave, but Elias stops them by placing a hand on Mom's arm. She looks down at where he's touching her, but doesn't have time to pull away before Elias whispers something in her ear. She doesn't seem pleased at all and I can't say I'm not happy about it.

"Have a great night," he says after stepping back to my side.

They hurry away, Mom leaning into Dad, probably telling him what Elias said to her.

"I don't even want to know," I laugh and point towards the bar.

He follows me, not once taking his hand from the small of my back as we make our way across the room. I try to walk faster, only to get back at him for what he did to me on the dance floor, but he squeezes my waist and keeps up with me.

We sit down on stools at the crystal-encrusted bar and I order drinks for the both of us. A Hugo cocktail for me and a red wine for him. He seems like the type to drink it.

Our drinks arrive pretty quickly, but I'm startled to see him refusing his and ordering a bottle of water instead.

"Wait." I stop the barman with a raise of my hand, while my eyes are glued to Elias. "Why?"

He shrugs and I pout. I always grab a drink when Mom

doesn't pay attention, although tonight feels different. I'm not drinking as a distraction, I'm drinking because tonight feels good.

"Who's going to drive?" he says.

Now it's my turn to shrug, absently playing with the straw in my drink. We can easily call an Uber, but I think it must be an excuse for him to get out of here sooner.

I always drink alone and I thought that today, maybe, I'd have someone to let loose with. I shake my head at my selfishness, knowing it wouldn't be fair to force him.

"You know what? Forget it," he says and moves his chair closer to mine. "Thank you." Elias says to the barman, picking up his wine.

I try to stop the smile from spreading across my face, but I can't help it. He smiles as well, and I take a sip from my drink.

"My dad used to drink a lot when I was little," he says.

The statement catches me off guard. Tom didn't seem like the type. Even imagining him having a drinking problem seems impossible. He looks healthy and happy, but I guess that's only the outcome of what he's been through.

"I try to avoid drinking as much as I can."

I nod, still looking down at my drink, feeling bad for making him keep his wine.

He places the tip of his index finger under my chin, lifting it and forcing me to make eye contact, then lowers his hand and grabs a hold of his drink, drawing circles with it on the counter.

"That period wasn't nice for any of us, and Mom hates the smell of alcohol."

He watches my reaction intently. I'm wearing my

lenses, but his gaze is strong enough to pierce through them.

Elias points towards my glass. I take a sip and he takes one. But it doesn't feel fun anymore. I don't want his mom to be mad at him and I definitely don't want to bring back bad memories.

"I'll finish this and then we can go. You should grab a water instead," I suggest.

He quickly dismisses it. "I'll just crash at a hotel."

"I'm serious. We can leave whenever."

Elias sighs, "And I'm serious, too. I can't remember the last time I had fun."

I nod. He's doing this just for me and I don't know how to take it yet. Feels weird. Not right.

"Cheers," Elias smiles, and I feel a fluttering in my chest.

"Cheers." I raise my Hugo and we clink our glasses together.

CHAPTER TWENTY FOUR
ELIAS

WE LEAVE MAYBE an hour or so later. Can't tell for sure. What I can tell is that we drank too damn much. At least I did, but Indigo seemed like she was familiar with her Hugo cocktail. I tell her as much.

"That's not true," she laughs, a hiccup leaving her lips, which makes me laugh too, although I can't remember what we're laughing about.

I open the cab door, letting her in first. Looks like even when drunk, I have manners. Elias: 1, Wine: 0. Indigo gets in, somehow managing to bump her head. She groans, cursing under her breath. Chuckling, I follow her in and pay extra attention to my head, which is a bad idea. With my whole attention on my head, I forget how high I have to raise my leg to get in. My shoe catches on the verge, making me lose my balance, so I tip forward and hit my chin on the seat.

Indigo bursts out laughing and slaps her thigh. I grunt in response. Getting back on my feet becomes really hard. I try to raise myself up, only to slip again, with my chin on the seat and my legs outside the vehicle.

"Stop laughing and help me," I say, but she just laughs harder and louder, her hands clutching her belly.

"Oh," she continues, wiping the tears from her eyes, "okay, okay."

I smile as I see her lean over, but right before she grabs my arm, she laughs again and opens her purse. She fishes out her phone.

"I have to take a picture." She laughs even harder, and it's contagious.

After taking a bunch of photos and making me laugh even more, she helps me get up.

"Where to?" the cab driver asks.

"How did he get here?" I ask Indigo, utterly confused, making her laugh again. I try to focus on her by squinting my eyes, but every time I try, my vision blurs.

"Home?" she asks, raising her arms in the air.

My head turns once again towards the driver. "You heard her," I nod, proud of myself. "We're going home."

Yeah. That seems like a great idea. The man scowls.

"Is he going to kill us like in that bad horror movie?" I whisper, jerking my bruised chin towards him. It really hurts now I'm thinking of it. Indigo shudders beside me, and I throw a protective hand around her. He can slice my throat first, but until then, she's under my protection.

"I need the name of a street," the creepy guy says, "and I'm not going to kill you," he sighs, massaging his temples.

My head hurts so much. Indigo murmurs something and the cabbie starts to drive off.

My head is leaning on Indigo's shoulder, my gaze fixed on her hands.

"You have beautiful hands," I burble, taking one of them in mine.

"One time I thought about modeling," she confesses, and I nod.

Can't think of proper things she could model with her hands, so I keep my mouth shut. A chuckle escapes my lips, and it's too late to stop it.

"What? You're not the only one that thinks my hands are pretty."

They look so smooth that I take one and brush it over my cheek, smiling at the feeling.

"What did you tell my mom to make her disappear so fast?" she suddenly asks while her palm is on my face.

I giggle and raise my head, looking her dead in the eye.

"That the only place you have fat is your ass."

WE SOMEHOW MANAGED to stop only once on the way back to her place, and that was because I felt the sudden urge to throw up. It turned out to be a false alarm, but I swear to God it was close.

Now we're laid out on her huge couch, head to head, with our legs sprawled towards each end

"I think it's time to get a place for myself," I say. It's crossed my mind so many times in the past few weeks. I can't stay in my parents' house forever.

"That actually sounds fun," she says.

I sit up properly and turn to her, and she does the same.

Now we're finally sitting like normal people.

"Really?"

"Yeah. I moved here three years ago and I've loved every second of it," Indigo declares, putting her head on a cushion.

I nod, remembering the first time I moved. "I hated it when I left home, but studying meant a lot to me, so I did it, anyway." It's actually hard to admit that I never wanted to leave home. Sounds like I'm a momma's boy. Can't say that I'm not.

"Hated leaving the town or your parents' house?"

"Both. But the second time I moved I was pretty excited. Moving in with Ava felt like the greatest change." I smile ironically at that.

"Why did you split up?"

I shrug. "We realized one of us wanted the relationship more than the other."

She nods, her eyes almost closing. I look at my watch, concentrating on it for a couple of seconds until my vision finally focuses. 3.30 AM.

Her head falls and she relaxes back on the couch. I decide to carry her upstairs, but when I try to get up, my legs are like jelly.

I look around and find a blanket. Grabbing it with shaky hands, I place it over her, getting a soft growl.

I stretch out on the huge sofa and yawn. "Do you want to go apartment hunting with me?" I whisper, not sure if she'll hear me.

"Mhmm," she murmurs, turning.

"Okay." My voice cracks and my eyes close, sleep finally taking me.

CHAPTER TWENTY FIVE
INDIGO

My body has never felt this weird.

It wants food, but it doesn't because every time I eat something I barf it up a minute later. It wants water, but that makes my tummy feel funny. It wants sleep, but when I try to, I feel vomit rising in my throat.

I usually drink enough to feel dumb. Yesterday, I drank enough to become a whole new person.

The toilet seat supports my cheek as I puke out all the Hugos. I locked the bathroom door so Elias would stop insisting on helping me. I can throw up on my own, thanks.

Can't say it worked. He still knocks on the door every two minutes. And my temples hurt so much from the banging that I want to drown in the toilet. A groan slips from my lips as I lift my head too quickly.

"Open the door," he says, knocking again. I shake my head at no one.

I stand on wobbly legs and look in the mirror. The reflection isn't that bad. Some dark bags under my eyes.

Messy hair, but it's like that most days. Probably the worst thing is my breath.

I turn on the water and wash my face as the knocking continues. "Go use the one upstairs!"

He still knocks, not giving a fuck about my headache. I growl and brush my teeth, tie my hair in a new bun, dry my hands, and open the door with a loud bang.

And there he is, lying on the floor, two cups of tea and some painkillers next to him. He smiles, his bruised chin showing.

I clear my throat and close the door behind me. "You should've drunk yours. I'm sure it's cold now."

He nods. "We got drunk together; we fight the hangover together."

"Yeah."

My body slides down until it lands on the floor beside him, and I take a sip of the tea, gripping the cup in my hands.

"Well, yesterday was a blast," he laughs.

I eye him curiously. He got drunk for my sake, waited for me as I puked my guts up, dressed in the same clothes as the previous day, and even made me some tea.

Things feel weird for some reason. Last night was fun, I have to admit that, but he's casual about everything, while I'm overthinking it all.

"So, hand model, huh?" he mocks.

Groaning, I hit my head on the wall. Why did I tell him that? He's not going to let it go.

PART TWO

TWO MONTHS LATER

CHAPTER TWENTY SIX
INDIGO

ELIAS and I have fallen into a routine over the last few weeks. Me, visiting his parents and helping him find a home, and him, attending every party without complaint. He didn't even snarl about the exhausting shopping day I put him through.

Elias was great at supporting me in front of my mom. It's strange, but at the same time, it feels good to know someone has my back.

I still haven't given him his jacket back; I like to wear it from time to time, even though the weather is getting warmer. I tell myself the only reason I wear it is because it's comfy.

Touching has also become a normal thing for us. His hand lingering on my leg, especially when we're driving to his house, or running my hand through his hair on the rare occasions we spend the night at his parents' house. And there's been plenty of stolen glances.

I think that's just because we're getting used to each

other. We're on good terms. Feeling comfortable around him has been easy, but good things never last.

"I really hope this is the one," I say as I drag myself onto the front porch.

This must be the third house we've visited today and the twentieth this week. He's too damn picky. *It doesn't have this, why does it have that, hate the placement, too expensive, too cheap.*

Elias chuckles as a petite lady opens the door.

"Hello, I'm Cora," she says, smiling at me then moving her gaze to Elias.

We shake hands, exchange names, and make our way inside. She shows us a stunning white kitchen, not too modern or too old-fashioned, with a big dining table in the center.

I can picture the entire Madden family here, and by the sparkle in Elias's eyes when he turns to see my reaction, I think he can too. We nod to each other and he moves his attention back to the realtor.

The kitchen and the living room are open-plan, similar to his parents' house. The couch is pretty ugly, but he can always change it, and there's space for a TV and PlayStation in front of it. I can easily picture him on the sofa, watching some plant documentary, his dog next to him.

I was surprised when I found out he has a dog. His name is Avocado, apparently because Elias loves avocados. As simple as that. He's a big golden retriever that loves hugs and licking people's faces.

He's become a big part of my life, just like his owner. I hadn't even realized it until this morning when Enya smiled proudly at me and said she's happy I finally found something to keep me busy.

Elias definitely keeps me busy. He's part of my everyday, whether I like it or not. I can't remember when I started feeling like I have no other choice than to be around him.

But I can totally recall the day Avocado and I met. It was actually the day after we got *way* too drunk and we went to his parents' for dinner. He said Avocado was the reason he left town. I didn't ask more questions, I just let the dog throw himself at me and cover me in kisses.

"When can I move in?" Elias suddenly asks, shaking me from my memories and surprising Cora, who hadn't even finished her tour.

It doesn't surprise me that Elias likes it. It's right by his parents' neighborhood and has everything you need nearby.

"Uh..." Cora was definitely not expecting that. "Today?" She shrugs, looking through her papers.

Elias nods and sighs in relief. He puts his hands on his hips while he takes a moment to look around him.

"The smile on your face creeps me out." I cringe and he chuckles, making my heart beat a little faster.

"Come over here. You have to see it from where I'm standing." He motions for me to join him and I cross the room.

He's got a point. From where we're standing, the beautiful kitchen is to our left, the ugliest couch on earth is in front of us, and a couple of shelves are to the right.

"So, what do you think?" He turns to me, looking directly into my eyes. It feels like he can see into my soul.

I shrug, not really knowing what to say. "As long as you like—"

"I asked what *you* think." His eyebrows shoot up.

Cora excuses herself, telling us she'll get the paperwork in order. We both nod and as soon as she's gone Elias pierces me with his gaze again.

I saved up all the money earned from my practice just for this moment. To look at my house.

"I love it," I say, "but this couch is fucking hideous."

Elias laughs at that, nodding in agreement. Well, I'm glad we're on the same page about that.

"Like really ugly," he says.

"So ugly," I whisper when I hear Cora approaching.

We all sit down on the awful couch for the next thirty minutes. Elias signs the papers and Cora talks about the next steps, which are pretty easy to follow. Since he's buying it, he can do whatever he wants with it.

Cora sits up, a contented smile on her face. "Well, that was the fastest sale I've ever had."

Elias laughs and leads her to the exit, where we say our goodbyes.

"It was nice meeting you," he declares and closes the door.

He turns and faces me with the biggest grin on earth. His happiness is so contagious that I can't stop my own smile from spreading across my face.

"I want to paint something in the little room," he states, his eyes sparkling.

"Then do it," I tell him. "It's your house."

"It's my house."

I look at the door to the little room, about to suggest going in, when his enormous arms grab my legs and raise me in the air. A high-pitched scream of surprise escapes me.

"It's my damn house," he shouts happily.

My hands go to his shoulders for stability, and I look down at his lips.

"It's your house," I mumble.

He stops moving, his gaze dropping from my eyes to my mouth. I swallow while he slowly puts me down. Neither of us makes a move, and I'm grateful for it. It's his turn to swallow as I gently land on my feet.

My palms are on his chest and his hands are on my back. When we finally make eye contact, it's devastating. The urge to fill the silence and break the moment takes over me, showing me how little progress I've actually made.

"What do you want to paint?" I gabble and he seems utterly confused. "On the wall I mean."

"Oh." He clears his throat and takes a step back. "A tree."

I hate how disappointed he looks and how cold I feel as he takes another step back. I close my eyes and take a deep breath.

Going to therapy has become a weekly thing for me, and, as my therapist told me, other people shouldn't be hurt by my lack of communication. I'm doing my best to put that into practice.

"I—," I start and open my eyes to see Elias raising his gaze from the floor, "I'm not rejecting you, Elias."

It's hard looking him straight in the eyes, but I want to do it. He seems taken aback.

"It's called self-sabotage," I admit and he nods. There's a moment or two of silence where we just watch each other, gazes burning skin.

"So? Do you think Livy is going to love it?" he says,

changing the topic and once again surprising me with how patient he is.

Despite the fact that he's had numerous occasions over the past few weeks, Elias has never pushed me beyond what I feel comfortable doing. He's let me speak if I've wanted to or stay silent if needed. I'm thankful for the way he's handling things, but I know he'll be done with them soon. It's only a matter of time.

So instead of torturing him with moments when I forget important things, when I cry my heart out for no reason, or when I get frustrated and angry, moments when I don't want to speak with anyone, when I can't even get a word out, I choose to let him free.

He doesn't need me as a burden. I shouldn't have let things get where they are now. To us being close, to him being the first person I speak to in the mornings, to me growing attached to him and his family.

And I have no way out.

CHAPTER TWENTY SEVEN

ELIAS

I LOOK DOWN at Indigo as she dips the brush into the paint can.

Yesterday we brought the majority of my stuff here. It was exhausting for both of us. We finished late last night and started early this morning, and Indigo, who isn't a morning person, didn't even complain.

Actually, she talked less than usual.

I can't always tell what's happening in that head of hers, but one thing I know is that she's lost in her thoughts, and as much as I try to get her out of them, she keeps dragging herself right back.

It must be about the kiss that almost happened. What excuse could I possibly give her? *Sorry, I got too excited and carried away? Oh, that wasn't even my intention.*

Because that means lying. I mean, yes, I was thrilled, but the excitement will never dictate my feelings. Especially toward her.

"Hey," I raise my chin at her, along with my cup of coffee, trying to get her attention.

She's gotten really into painting the tree on the wall. I didn't know she was this talented, but apparently she used to do it a lot in her high school years.

"Yeah?" She moves her gaze to me. She's kneeling, brush still dipped in paint.

"Can we...?" I scratch the back of my head, avoiding eye contact. "Can we talk?"

Surprise flashes in her eyes, and she blinks it away before nodding. She gets up and follows me into the lounge area, where we both sit on the couch.

I sigh, not wanting to make this awkward. "I don't want things to be weird between us."

And it's true. Things were amazing. She started speaking more, making jokes, and having fun. She's gradually learning to trust people, which is a significant improvement in how she was on the day we met.

"Me neither," she shakes her head, clearly weighed down by something.

Indigo started to see a therapist last month, and they've really helped her progress. I'm not supposed to know about it, but Liv told me so I'd be patient with her. I don't see it that way, though. I don't need to be patient with Indigo. After a day spent with her, I'm never tired or eager to get home. Quite the opposite.

She's still human. Why treat her differently when what she clearly wants is normalcy?

While I still don't know why it's so hard for her to communicate and express her feelings, she's clearly working hard to get there.

"Why the cold shoulder?" I ask. "Is it because of us almost kissing?" I go straight to the point. I don't try to beat around the bush. An article on the internet said that when people speak to a person with social anxiety, they tend to wrap things in a pretty package, which is the last thing you should do. It's best to show them the reality.

She takes a deep breath, bites her lower lip, and nods.

"I'm sorry." I lower my head, feeling guilty for her attitude these past few days. "I didn't mean to make you uncomfortable."

"It's not your fault."

We stare at each other as she struggles to find the words for whatever she's holding inside.

And I wait.

I let her look at me, analyze my entire face, my body language, anything that would give her the time to think and rethink before finally speaking. When it comes to me, Indigo has all the time in the world and more. It's just that she doesn't know it yet.

She lets out a frustrated laugh, massaging her temples with the tips of her fingers. Her hands tremble and although my body hurts from working all day, I don't relax back into the couch, afraid that any movement could make her take a step back.

"It's scary," she whispers, a tremor in her voice.

"Us kissing?"

Indigo raises her head from her palms. "Yeah." She shrugs, gaze on the ceiling.

We sit quietly. Me looking at her, grateful she isn't wearing her contacts so I can see her true self, and Indigo looking everywhere but me.

"I wanted to kiss you too," she mumbles, glancing at me.

A little smile finds its way to my face. "Is it bad now it's real?"

I'd hate to hear her say yes, and that terrifies me. It's been a little over half a year since Ava and I broke up, but we never had to work on our relationship. We were just together.

"It's scary," she repeats, finally facing me.

"It is." I nod, thinking the same.

"But this," she points between us, back and forth, "will only make things complicated."

"Maybe."

I don't want to tell her things will definitely work because I don't know that. The only thing I do know is that I wanted to kiss her and that I won't refuse her if the opportunity ever comes again.

However, I could never forgive myself if I'd tried to convince her to do something too quickly. I just knew that I wanted to kiss her. I never thought past that at the time.

"What?" She looks surprised. "Imagine us breaking up while I still have to be your fake girlfriend and you my fake boyfriend."

"You're trying to talk yourself out of this," I say.

"No... What? I'm not." She takes a deep breath then edges closer to me, keeping her hands on her legs. "What do *you* think?"

"I don't know." I shrug. "I left my pros and cons list at home."

That earns me a laugh, which makes me feel a bit better.

"I'm serious. I want to know your opinion on this."

"I don't know, Indigo." And it's true. "When I feel something, I just do it without asking myself why or what the repercussions will be, because I'll never regret doing it. Especially kissing you. People kiss every day, and most of them don't even feel like doing it, so I'd say that both of us wanting to is a pretty good start."

She smiles softly at me and without thinking about it too much, I open my arms for her. "Come here."

Judging by the look on her face, she isn't necessarily happy to do it. She does it anyway, her intoxicating smell embracing me, along with the warmth of her body. This just feels right.

"I don't think I'm ready for a commitment," Indigo honestly declares. "There are already too many changes in my life, and this would be a major one."

"Okay," I whisper, knowing that if it's meant to be, then it'll happen eventually. "Thank you for talking with me."

She nods in my arms, a sigh escaping her lips. I hope this conversation helped her with the consuming thoughts.

It certainly made me think about it more and I've realized the urge to kiss her didn't just come from excitement.

CHAPTER TWENTY EIGHT
INDIGO

Admitting my feelings made things more real. While Elias seems unbothered by it, I'm freaking out, over-thinking it as usual. I don't know how someone can be so calm about something that complicates things that are already complicated.

That's precisely why I'm here, two days early for my therapy appointment. Darla is a brilliant, gentle woman, but she pushes my buttons a *lot*. Every week, she gives me a new challenge I must achieve before our next session.

I know her methods work, but the tasks only get harder, and now I need to come here twice a week because I feel like I'm going crazy.

"I really can't understand where the problem is." She shrugs, sitting in her big black chair behind her desk, playing with a pen between her fingers.

My mouth falls open. "What do you mean *you don't know what the problem is*? Can't you see how fucked up all of this is?" I shift in my seat, avoiding eye contact.

She smirks, finding my cursing funny. I wouldn't be

Indigo without it. It always adds a little bit of spark to things.

Darla places her elbows on the large desk, rests her head on her hands, and peers at me closely. "On that, I'm with you," she smiles, "but we have to be honest and admit that if it wasn't for this whole arrangement, you wouldn't be here today."

I reluctantly nod in agreement. It's true. If it wasn't for Olivia and Elias, I would still be in bed most days, watching TV and eating popcorn. It's just that it doesn't feel real anymore. I can still remember the days I was doing nothing more than staying in, and I was okay with that. The story isn't the same anymore.

"You're progressing, Indigo." She puts her hand on top of mine and a tear escapes me. "You really are, and I'm proud of you for it."

I swallow the lump in my throat and do nothing but nod. What else could I do or say?

"Why don't you take advantage of this opportunity?"

A bitter laugh finds its way out of my tight chest. My life isn't a fucking game and I honestly don't understand how she thinks this is easy. This isn't easy at all.

"This seems like an opportunity to you?" I snap, although it wasn't my intention. I take my hand from under hers, and she only smiles at me.

"Life is too short to see it otherwise. You need to understand that. Why won't you give it a try? You said he is funny, honest, and patient." She inclines her head, watching me with intense blue eyes. "So what if he isn't the one? He's here for a reason, and I think he's a big part of your healing process."

Tears fall from my eyes and I don't even bother to cover them. "Are you all so blind to how hard I'm trying?" I whisper.

Darla seems taken aback, hurt by my words. "No, Indigo," she starts, "look at me." She puts her finger under my chin, raising it and forcing me to meet her eyes. "I've never said that, okay?"

I ignore her question and cover my face with my hands, my chest feeling heavy.

"Think about where you were two months ago, then one month ago, then two weeks ago. Indigo, you don't even realize how brave you were for telling him how you feel. Not many people can do that."

I know she's right, there is progress, but everything seems to get harder and harder.

"I hate the way I am, and I don't know how to stop it," I mumble into my hands. She slowly pulls them away from my face, revealing the tears that continue to slide down my cheeks.

"Nothing. Is. Wrong with you." She takes a piece of paper and writes something on it, and I know it's game over. That's another task. "This week you are going to live," Darla says while writing with her fancy pen.

I sigh, not entirely ready for whatever she has prepared. She's always so inspired to give me tasks. I wonder when they're going to stop. She'll finally run out of ideas, right?

"Your homework for the next week is to do everything impulsively." She hands me the pink sticky note. "If your first thought is to sleep instead of going somewhere, do it. If your gut tells you to kiss a guy, kiss him. No overthinking is allowed."

I growl at her, and she only laughs as I look down at the note. Her cursive writing says, *Better regret something you did than regret something you didn't.* Sighing, I nod, knowing she's right.

But what if this week will change my life in a bad way? My thoughts are chaotic and if I follow them then maybe I'll end up with a dog, although I know I'm not responsible enough to take care of him or even—

"Stop it," she snaps, shoving her pen at me.

"Ugh." I bang my head on the desk.

"Do you want to live happily?"

I raise one eyebrow, not understanding. "Of course I want that. Who wouldn't?"

"Then fucking do it," she says, clearly.

I laugh. "Don't swear, it sounds weird coming from you." Darla is a rainbow girl. She actually reminds me a lot of Olivia. She really knows how to live; she's told me a bit about her life. Darla has two kids, Karen and David, and a husband that would do anything for her. Including letting her practice her nail art on him.

"What? I was trying to be cool," she laughs, her face radiating.

I burst out laughing, praying to God she'll never do it again.

CHAPTER TWENTY NINE
ELIAS

ON MONDAY, Indigo and I finished painting Olivia's room and putting the rest of the house in place. It was a difficult job, especially because we haven't solved anything between us. The conversation we had a couple of days ago was meant to make her not overthink things.

Well, it didn't work. It seemed like she was hurrying to get the job done so she could run back to her bed.

Today is Wednesday, and I still haven't heard anything from her, and neither has Olivia. At first, I thought she needed some time alone, but she hasn't replied to any of our messages. That's what's prompted us to drive to her house and check if she still has a pulse.

Olivia gets out of the car first and I follow her, fiddling with the hem of my shirt. From the time I've spent with Indigo, I know she disappears occasionally, but she's always replied to Olivia's calls, if not mine. And I'd be less worried if Indigo hadn't been acting weirdly beforehand.

Olivia looks back at me when we get to the front porch and I nod, encouraging her to knock. She does and a second later we hear something crash to the floor, followed by Indigo's curses.

"Damn it," she says. "I'm coming!"

Our shoulders drop in relief and we smile at each other. The stream of curses continues until Indigo opens the door. She has a big bun on top of her head, large dark circles under her eyes, a white, over-sized t-shirt that falls to her thighs, and a long pair of socks.

"Oh." Her eyes lock with mine and then Olivia's. "What happened? Actually, what day is it?" She frowns, looking at the sky like it would give her an answer.

"Wednesday," I growl. She seems spaced out. The idea of her being on drugs makes my blood run cold.

"Can we come in?" Olivia doesn't wait for her to reply, she just barges past.

Indigo follows her, looking lost in her own place. I step inside and stop in my tracks as soon as I see the mess. And not only that, a puppy is ripping up the couch pillows while another spreads her makeup on the white fluffy rug.

"What the..." I mumble, my voice fading away as I analyze everything that's happening.

Indigo nods, exhaustion on her features. She drops on the sofa and pulls her scrunchie from her hair. Olivia gasps and I almost do too.

Her long hair is now much shorter, just touching her shoulders. I can't stop staring at it.

She notices our gaze and shifts uncomfortably in her seat, threading her fingers through it.

"What?" she shrugs, looking everywhere but us.

I don't even try to form a response, I only stare at how different she looks with it cut this short. Good different. It brings her eyes into focus and makes her high cheekbones even more contoured.

One of the dogs jumps at me and sniffs, probably picking up the scent of Avocado. I hardly take my eyes off Indigo. The two puppies play around my legs while I pet them and tell them how good they are. One of them is a Labrador and the other is a golden retriever. Just like Avocado.

I look up at Indigo and a soft smile forms on her lips. Olivia still looks shocked. I follow her gaze and notice the wall behind Indigo is painted black.

"Did something happen?" I ask, truly concerned.

Indigo shakes her head. I look at Olivia and she looks at me. We nod to each other and sit on either side of Indigo.

"You guys are acting weird," she comments, looking from me to Livy.

"What happened?" Olivia demands.

Indigo shrugs. "Darla forced me to see things differently, and at first I refused to do it, but then I had a fight with Mom and ended up like this." She throws her head back on the sofa and groans.

"I understand the black wall, you needed the change," Livy says, "but what's up with the dogs?"

I'm surprised she doesn't ask about Indigo's fight with her mom. That would be the first thing I'd ask. If that's what triggered all this, we have to go to the source.

The puppies bark and nip at each other's ears, running in circles and knocking some candles off the table. I chuckle, pat them as they race past, and replace the candles.

As I look back at Indigo, I notice she's falling asleep.

Her mouth is parted, each breath she takes sounds like a sigh.

"I'll take her upstairs," I whisper.

Livy nods. "I'll clean up in here."

I slowly wiggle one arm under Indigo's knees, one under her shoulders, and lift her carefully. She murmurs something and I stop, giving her time to snuggle into me, which makes carrying her much easier.

She isn't heavy. She must weigh about the same as Avocado. I carry him almost every night, and Indigo doesn't feel much different.

When we get to the top of the stairs, I'm relieved to see her door already ajar. I push it open with my foot and step in. The floor is covered in clothes. A few sketches are scattered here and there. Because of the angle, I can't see what the drawings are, but I'm intrigued.

I gently put her down on the king size bed and gaze at her face. Even this tired, she takes my breath away. I knew when I met her that Indigo was a beautiful woman.

After arranging her head on the pillow and covering her with a blanket, I sit on the edge of the bed and watch her for a couple of seconds.

Indigo and I are nothing, and at the same time, we're everything. We're complicated and we still haven't named whatever we are, because in theory, we're a fake couple that enjoys each other's company.

I must admit that until recently, I've never thought of her as more than a friend. I've always seen her as a beautiful woman, and I still do, but the past couple of weeks have changed something.

My mind has no clarity, but I know that if she tried to

kiss me, I'd let her. I know that if she asked me to do something for her, I'd do it without hesitation. I can't decide if that freaks me out or not.

She shifts and half opens her eyes. Eyes that I can't stop staring at. Normally, I'd feel awkward and excuse myself, but nothing in her expression tells me to leave.

So I stay.

And Indigo watches me.

"I told my mom I'm not attending the party this Sunday. Or ever," she whispers.

My heart warms at her confiding in me. I don't know what pushes me to do it, but I brush her hair behind her ear. She shivers at my touch, but says nothing.

"How did that go?" I ask.

"It sucked. She emptied all my bank accounts." She shrugs, trying to act like she doesn't care, but I can tell she does.

"I'm sure you have some money set aside." Encouraging her seems like the best thing to do, as this is such a big change in her life. I know how it felt for me to leave my parents' protection — it wasn't pretty. Worked two jobs all my university years, slept, and studied.

"I do, but it's more complicated than that," she says, shifting slightly. I realize I've been unconsciously playing with her hair. I pull my hand away.

"Is this house in your name?" I don't know why I ask this. I regret it with my whole heart when her face drops.

"No," she says, turning her back to me.

My mind is empty. I don't know what to say to make it better. "I'm sure she isn't going to throw her daughter out on the streets," I mumble. The urge to slap myself is unbearable.

Indigo sniffles, "Yeah." By the way she says it, something makes me think her mom would throw her out in an instant.

By the time I think to tell her that my place is free whenever she needs it, her breath has evened and I realize she's fallen into a deep sleep.

CHAPTER THIRTY
INDIGO

SHORT HAIR SUITS ME. There's something about it, but I can't put my finger on it. It makes me look powerful, confident. A whole new person. I guess that's what I wanted: a new identity. Even though cutting my hair won't give me that.

I put my hands on the edge of the bathroom sink and gaze at my reflection. Knowing that Grandma's house isn't in my name makes it harder to free myself from Mom's grasp.

The truth is, I knew this from the start. Nothing is in my name. If I was doing whatever she wanted, then I was supported financially and given a home. A home that carries all my beautiful memories.

My grandma was my only friend. She was a great listener. I know she felt responsible for everything that happened to me, but it wasn't her fault. She wasn't responsible for her daughter's actions.

We would always cuddle in her tiny bed and watch soap operas. I was totally hooked on them. I guess that's where I got my obsession with TV. And she loved to wash my hair, even though her back hurt. And she'd cook mashed potatoes for me, no matter the hour, just because she knew I loved them.

She taught me this recipe to do when I crave something sweet. It's so simple — just white bread, sugar, and a couple of drops of water. I know it sounds weird, but it's the best thing I've ever tasted.

Her name was Maria, and she was a light in my life. Until she passed away.

I sniffle, noticing the tears on my cheeks. Wiping them away, I open the bathroom door and walk downstairs. If this is my last day in this house, I can't leave without a meal in Grandma's honor.

As I reach the bottom, I'm surprised to see Elias asleep on the couch, his body almost falling to the floor and one of his big hands plastered to his chest. Dog One is asleep under his arm, while Dog Two is nuzzling his hair.

I snap a photo with my phone, then quietly cover him with a blanket, praying to God I won't wake him up. He looks at peace, his face all relaxed.

My gaze finds its way to his lips. They look more full than usual. I lean forward, closing the distance between us, then take a step back when I realize how stupid this is. I pick at my cuticles and consider my next move.

I close my eyes and sigh.

Fuck it.

I lean forward again and kiss him. Quickly. Almost like a peck. I turn, ready to leave, when a warm hand grasps my arm. I freeze, too afraid to move. Maybe if I stay still, he'll think it's a dream. Yeah. Sounds like a plan.

"One more." His raspy voice fills the silence.

I find the courage to face him. He can barely keep his eyes open, and yet he still hasn't let go of my hand. A soft smile plays on the lips I kissed just seconds ago.

I swallow the lump in my throat, scanning his features. He looks so damn relaxed while I'm so close to freaking out. His ability to be this carefree makes me envious.

He tugs on my hand and I lower my face so our lips are close to touching. He smells like summer grass and I love it. He doesn't make a move, just keeps his mouth close to mine. I daren't move.

My breath catches, and he stops breathing. We just stare at each other's lips and I feel my heart thudding in my chest. His hand goes to the back of my head and he presses his forehead to mine.

A frustrated growl is all I hear before his mouth smashes into mine and his fingers clutch at my hair. His kiss is unexpectedly passionate. He doesn't ask, he just takes it.

His roughness makes me moan and the pit of my stomach falls into a wild swirl. Any calm that was in me before, shatters with the hunger of his kiss.

The dogs take it as their cue to leave when he grabs me by my waist and pulls me on top of him, not once breaking the closeness of our lips.

Elias doesn't seem to care about taking it slow. His hands roam all over my body, squeezing my ass with his hands. My back arches in response, earning a masculine groan from him.

His groin pushes into my center and the urge to grind against him shakes me to the core.

A hot tide of passion rips through me. We break to take

a breath and the separation hurts. My heartbeat throbs in my ear as I look down at his moist red lips.

His chest rises and falls with fast breaths. I look down at mine and notice I'm panting too.

"See?" he whispers. "This is what you do to me. You take my breath away."

I shift. His words sound strange. Not because I don't like them, but because they seem too big to say yet. My movement only takes me closer to his crotch. I sit straight on him and I register the hardness beneath me.

He chuckles. "And that."

That makes the tension in my shoulders ease a little and I let out a laugh.

His face drops a little as he says, "Do you regret it?" Green eyes full of hope bore into mine and set my soul alight.

I take his question seriously. I don't want to lie to him, so I take a few moments to think about it, even knowing that every second that passes must feel like an eternity to him.

My only question is: what could go wrong? And the answer is: nothing. No more overthinking. No more creating fake scenarios in my head. This is real.

"No," I say.

He sighs, dropping his head to my shoulder. When he glances back, he sees me smiling, and his brow furrows.

"Was that funny to you?" He sounds so serious that my mind screams danger and wipes the smile off my face.

"No," I respond. He raises an eyebrow. "Definitely not." I shake my head, trying to be clear.

A smirk slowly reaches his lips and I smack his arm, laughing along with him.

"It wasn't funny," he says, grabbing me and kissing my forehead. "I was ready for you to run back to your room."

I relax under his embrace and mumble, "Not anymore."

His kiss was destined for my tired soul to melt into. He gently took it when it was stuck in darkness, gave it time and caressed it until it started to show signs of light.

For the first time in my life, a hug doesn't make me feel like whirling on my legs and dashing away. And as much as I'd like to stay like this forever, I have to pack. I decided to leave before my parents get the chance to throw me out, plus, I already know what terms we settled on.

And I need to eat a meal in honor of my last day in Grandma's house. I untangle myself from his embrace, explaining what I need to do, and make my way to the kitchen where he follows me.

I grab a loaf of bread and tear off the ends, one for me and one for him. If he doesn't want it, then that just means more for me. I scoop the crumbs out, then put a spoon of sugar in each.

If he thinks this is weird, he doesn't show it. He just takes a seat and watches me. I pour in a bit of water, just enough to soften it, and give one to him. He eyes me suspiciously but takes it.

As soon as I take a bite, my eyes fill with tears. It reminds me so much of Grandma.

He tastes it and his eyes widen. "Mmm," he mumbles through the crumbs.

"I know," I say and take a seat next to him.

"This is oddly good," he admits, taking another bite.

"Haven't eaten one of these since I was a kid."

Elias grabs my chair and pulls me closer, like the centimeters between us were too much. He puts a hand on my leg while we eat in silence.

I look at my watch and realize it's already eight in the morning. I know he and Olivia came at about seven last night. As I look around, I realize the place is gleaming. Swallowing the last bite, I gesture at the surroundings.

"Thank you."

He leans over and simply kisses me in reply.

CHAPTER THIRTY ONE
ELIAS

"Nothing. Fucking nothing," Indigo says as she paces back and forth, the dogs running around after her.

I sigh, massaging my temples with the tips of my fingers. "I told you already—"

"No," she cuts me off, raising her phone to her ears. After numerous shakes of her leg and impatient sighs, the person on the other end answers. She lays out the same speech she's said to every other agency she's called today, and by the look on her face, their response is the same.

It's hard to buy a house on the same day you want to move. Before I visited my new house for the first time, I spoke with the agency a week in advance. Sure, there are a lot of houses for sale right now, but few of them are available immediately.

When Indigo ends the call, Enya grabs her by the shoulders, forcing her to listen. I watch from the couch.

"You're always more than welcome at my house," she says, but Indigo just shakes her head.

"Why are you so stubborn?" I ask.

She shrugs and throws herself on the sofa, groaning, surely exhausted from the one hundred calls she's made today.

"You can either go to Enya's or my place until you find something."

"No, I can't."

Her answer frustrates me so much that I want to kiss it off her lips. "Why?" I fight back.

"Because Enya wouldn't last a week with me. She has two kids and I have two dogs. Kai is allergic to dog hair."

"We could make it work," Enya pushes.

"Fair enough," I agree with Indigo, "but why wouldn't my place work?"

She laughs sarcastically, turning to face me. She opens and closes her mouth a couple of times. "Because..." she begins, but changes her mind.

Enya sits down next to us and pats Indigo's leg, a sympathetic look on her face.

"You have Avocado," Indigo says.

"He loves making friends."

"I'm messy."

"I'll clean."

"So messy." She leans over, her brows furrowing.

"That's it?" I ask, not impressed by her motives.

All this stress has quickly washed away the lightness that was between us this morning. I can see how tired she is. We've spent over eight hours packing and we're still not done.

"We've barely even kissed," she cracks a sarcastic laugh. "I can't move in with you for obvious reasons."

I groan. "Why are we talking about the kiss?" She

shoots daggers with her eyes, but I ignore them. "Do you have another place to stay?"

"No."

"Exactly. Stop being stubborn and accept my help."

"Your help would speed things up between us. I don't want to go any faster."

Indigo's chin touches her chest while she plays with her cuticles. I glance at Enya, whose eyes widen as she signs at me to say something.

"This is not permanent," I say. "You can find a place to stay in less than a week. I can talk to that realtor, Cora, if you want." I look at Enya for confirmation. She nods, eyeing Indigo.

"Yeah. I know," Indigo replies absently. "There are just too many things going on and moving in with you doesn't seem like the right choice. I can sleep at a hotel."

"No," both Enya and I reply.

"It's time to take your life into your own hands," the older woman says, caressing Indigo's hair to relax her.

She sighs and nods reluctantly. "I'm not going to cook."

"Okay."

"Or wash your clothes." She points at me and I let out a laugh, raising my arms in mock surrender.

She grabs her phone and calls the removal company. Enya and I exchange looks, neither of us sure of how this will go.

CHAPTER THIRTY TWO
INDIGO

ELIAS IS IN HIS ROOM, getting some work done, while I sit on the ugly couch, watching a new Netflix movie. I have to admit that it's pretty good so far. Feels like my life with all the fake relationships and shit.

Most of my things are in a private lockup; I've just got the bare essentials here in the hope that I'll have my own place soon enough. For the past couple of days, Elias has slept on the couch. We've shared a bed at his parents' house, but this feels different. Maybe that's why he made a makeshift bed on the couch before I could say anything about it.

I'm really struggling to get back to normality, but then what is normality for me? Sitting on the couch all day, eating, sleeping, waking up, repeating? Hell no. I want to do more than that now, but I don't know what.

I want to paint again. The project in Olivia's room was a good start, but I'd like to do it for myself again, not just as a favor. But unfortunately, I have no motivation to do it. I don't know where to start or what to do. Drawing was a big thing for me in my high school years, but Mom made me stop. I've started and quit a lot of things because of her. It was like as soon as she sensed I was starting to love a hobby she took it away.

Dog One jumps on my legs, shaking me from my thoughts. I still haven't thought of names for them. I've looked for some on the internet, but they're all unoriginal.

Elias opens his bedroom door, and Avocado comes bounding out. He sniffs at the puppies, then jumps up to lick my face. Smiling, I pet him on the head, making him wag his tail happily.

"You hungry?" Elias casually asks, dressed in shorts and a T-shirt.

He really is a temptation.

I look him up and down and I nod, swallowing when he closes the distance and sits down next to me. He taps on his phone, searching through Uber Eats.

"I'm going to buy something for Olivia, too. She's staying the night, if you don't mind?" he asks, waiting for my confirmation.

"What? No, this is your house, Elias," I laugh. I don't mind if Liv visits. Her presence will keep me from throwing myself at her brother.

Who knew perceptions could switch and change so fast? I've always known Elias is attractive, but the thought of kissing him rarely crossed my mind. At least not until a week ago. Now I notice every single thing about him.

I noticed how his nose twitches whenever he's uncomfortable or how he licks his lips when they're dry. I noticed how most of his t-shirts are white, and he doesn't care about the state of his pants. I glance at them now and wonder —

"As long as you're here, it's your house too," he says, shaking me from that train of thought. "I've ordered pizza for us all." He puts his phone down and sighs.

Elias takes his glasses off — he only wears them when he's working — and massages his temples with his fingers.

"What?" I ask. "Work didn't go as planned?"

He shakes his head. "It's great, actually. I have a meeting with a well-known doctor, so no. It's not about that."

"What then?" I turn to him to give him my full attention.

"I'm nervous about how Olivia might react." He shrugs and I instantly smile. "What?" he asks.

"Nothing," I say. He raises a brow in question. "You're a good brother."

"Yeah, yeah."

I smack him on the arm. "I'm serious. I think she's going to love it."

He looks at me from one eye to the other. He seems to do it whenever I'm not wearing lenses. It's like he's taking the time to analyze them.

"I like you better this way." He brushes a couple of strands of hair behind my ear. "There's no barrier between you and me with your lenses off."

"Yeah," I whisper and he leans toward me, his eyes fixed on my lips.

Avocado and Dog One jump off the couch, sensing the mood changing.

"I like knowing I can kiss you anytime I want to," he admits, our mouths only millimeters apart.

Our lips brush and with one last swallow, I take what's mine. He groans and pulls me on top of him, forcing my legs to wrap around his torso. He pushes his hips upwards, finding my heat that already throbs for him. I shiver and bite his tongue after gently sucking it into my mouth.

He pins me to him, grabbing my hips so I can't move. I didn't even realize I was grinding on him. I wiggle in response — it's my turn to tempt him. For the past three days, this is all he's done to me: forgetting his T-shirt after a shower, getting out of the bath dressed only in a towel, or finding an excuse to take his shirt off.

"Please stop moving," he growls through gritted teeth.

"Make me," I challenge.

I don't know where all this confidence came from, but I like it. It makes me feel powerful. Dominant.

He lifts me up as if I weigh nothing at all and flips me over on my stomach. His large hands grip mine. I shiver and try to turn to look at him. It's almost impossible to do so from this position.

He lowers himself, his mouth tantalizing close to my ear. His breath tickles my neck and I hear him inhale as if he's about to say something, but the sound of someone fake barfing stops us in our tracks.

Elias looks up, not yet letting go of my hands.

"Ew," a young female voice says. Shitty timing, Olivia.

Elias lets me go and we stand up to see her putting a finger in her mouth while sticking her tongue out.

"Listen, I'm happy for you, but could we not let this

happen again? Like ever?" A disgusted look washes over her features and I just stand there, not saying a word.

"Yes, ma'am," Elias jokes, straightening his back like in the military. "Although maybe just knock next time."

"Ugh, my poor eyes." She hugs us both. "Why do you look like you're constipated?" she asks me.

I laugh at that, tensions easing. I feel bad for not telling her about us, but I don't even know what I could've said. Your brother and I kissed and this fake relationship might not be fake anymore? Or whatever this is?

We've never put a name to it. We haven't even had the time to. The last few days have passed in a blur of making out, work, and home hunting.

"I guess I'm just surprised to see you here so soon," I shrug.

We all laugh, and Elias puts his hand on the small of her back. "Come on, I want to show you something."

Olivia follows without complaint, and I amble behind. She turns to mouth *never again* at me. I chuckle and shake my head.

Elias stops in front of her bedroom door and encourages her to enter. She steps into the room and he flicks the lights on.

She gasps as her eyes fall on the mural of Mushroom, the three of us standing next to him. I felt like the picture needed something else besides the big tree, so I decided to paint the two of them. Then Elias insisted I include myself. He said Olivia would love to have me there as well.

A sob breaks out from her and she throws herself into her brother's arms. He laughs, hugging her back, then dragging me into the embrace with them. I try to pull away, but he only squeezes harder.

"Indigo painted it," he says.

Olivia looks up at me, her eyes sparkling with tears and surprise. "Thank you," she whispers and wraps an arm around me.

Elias kisses the top of her head and my heart melts.

CHAPTER THIRTY THREE

ELIAS

Indigo and I talk every night before bed. Once she's asleep, I quietly leave my room and lie on the couch. I end up staring at the ceiling most nights, wondering if I should sleep next to her. But then I remember that no matter how attracted I am to Indigo, and how painful it feels to be away from her, we need to take things slowly.

She just got out of the bathroom after taking a shower. I'm doing my best to neaten the covers and fluff her pillow, anything to distract me from thinking about what's underneath her shorts and T-shirt. She collapses on the bed and a quiet sigh escapes her lips as her body relaxes.

While I've been working on making tree therapy a real thing, Indigo has called a bunch of agencies and visited tons of places. She said there are lots available, but none of them felt like home. I can understand that, so I've reassured her she can stay until she finds something she loves.

"Did your mom call?" I ask, lying down next to her.

We're both on our backs, looking up at the ceiling. She turns her body to face me, and I do the same.

"No," she answers simply. She doesn't seem sad about it.

"Do you want her to call?" I ask out of curiosity.

"Not really."

I nod. I've never been through anything like this, but I can understand a little of what she's feeling. I try to put myself in her place. There must be a reason she doesn't want her mom around. Don't know much about her dad. He was pretty absent every time we met. They're kind of unpleasant people to be around.

"There's nothing you can do with your grandma's house? Like, buy it or something?"

"In theory, yeah, but it's much more than that." I can see how much this affects her and I wish I could make it better. "Plus, they'd never sell it to me because they know how much it means." She shrugs like it's nothing.

"Jesus," I whisper, threading my fingers through my hair. "Wait... what if I buy it?" The idea suddenly flicks into my mind.

"They know you already," she replies in an instant.

"I can speak with my dad or a friend of mine," I suggest, knowing they'd do it for me.

"We'd have to lie to your parents again, and I'm tired of it," she admits, a drained look on her face.

"Yeah, it sucks."

Soon, we're going to get lost in the lies we've told. Indigo has no grandmother living here, she doesn't own a big company, we're not in love. The only true thing is my feelings, and they're growing as we get to know each other better. Don't know where that will take us, but I know I don't want to lie anymore.

"Should we tell them the truth?" I ask.

She shrugs. "I don't know if I'm ready yet. Admitting we've been lying to them this whole time will be really tough."

I nod. "I could still speak with someone else."

"Nah," she shakes her head. "The house hasn't felt like hers since she's been gone, anyway."

I don't know much about Mushroom, just that he was her grandmother's, and the garden was a comforting place for her as a kid. Honestly, that's enough to make her feel this way. I can't imagine my house without the big family table or my childhood bedroom. They carry memories, and when you lose whatever keeps your memories alive, you start to feel like it never happened.

"I try not to think about it, you know?" She shrugs.

"Come here." I lie back and open my arm to her. She drags her body closer and puts her head on my chest and her hand on my stomach.

"Don't get used to it," she says when I kiss her head. She smells like cookies fresh from the oven. "I don't like hugs."

"Mhmm."

She looks up at me, her beautiful eyes piercing mine. I'll never get enough of them. "What?" she says.

I smirk. "You said the same thing about people, and you seem to like me just fine."

"That's because I have no other option," she challenges, raising her brows. "You are *so* invasive."

"Yeah?" I ask, ready to pin her down in less than a second.

"Mhmm," she starts before I throw her onto her front, picking up where we left off the other day.

I grab her hands and lie on top of her, so she can't move. She tries to turn to look at me, but she can barely raise her head. A playful smirk finds its way onto her face.

Seeing her this way makes me hard like stone, and I've barely even touched her. A growl escapes my throat as I lower my face to hers. I catch her ear lobe between my teeth. I don't bite it, just keep it there, letting my breath dance across her skin.

My heart has never beat this fast. I think I must've felt this way since I met her, I was just too blind to see it.

Her hands are now kept captive by only one of mine, while the other slowly traces her back. She shivers and I move my legs a little, giving me the freedom to grind my hips against her. Indigo mumbles something and presses herself back into me.

It feels so good that I almost come from that alone. I let out a guttural growl and Indigo moves under me. The friction is enough to make my eyes roll.

"If you want this to last more than a second, you have to stop moving like that."

She shakes her head, enjoying having me at her mercy. She continues to grind back on me and I only press harder, wishing there was no fabric between us.

Her breath shudders and I'm glad this affects her as much as it affects me.

"Indigo," I warn through gritted teeth.

I'm trying to keep myself from fully letting go, but she keeps growing greedier. She raises her hips a little higher so I can feel the warmth between her legs as she continues to grind against me. A moan escapes my lips as she changes her rhythm.

"You have to be quiet," she whispers through her own moans.

I grab her hair in a twist and I meet her thrust, both of us moving like crazy. Can't understand why we must be quiet, but I follow her orders because if she stops now, I'm a dead man walking.

The pressure becomes too much. Her curves bend and trap my mind, those shapely thighs and her satin soft skin making it impossible to keep my desire at bay.

She moans deep in her throat, holding back a whimper when I drop a soft kiss on her shoulder.

"Oh, fuck." A low rumble of pleasure slips past my lips. It's all so intense. Hearing her muffled sounds of pleasure and her growing needier tips me over the edge. My grasp on her hair slowly loosens as the only thing I know is her release and mine.

Our bodies continue to move together at a slow pace. We lock eyes, her face looking flushed while her legs shudder under me. We come down the hill together. Through clothes. Like horny teenagers.

"Always a temptation," I say, as my fingers go for her shorts, feeling her heat and wetness through the material.

Moving the shorts and then panties to the side, I slowly slip two fingers inside her. She sensually gasps, pushing herself back onto my hand. I keep moving them, slowly and deliberately, making her race for another orgasm.

She moans and it's the hottest sound I've ever heard. I want to play it on repeat for the rest of my life.

I slip my fingers out when she's close, only as a tease to

get back for the past few days. Before leaning down to kiss her, I allow myself a tiny taste of her juices. Sucking on my fingers, my shaft hardens again at the flavor of her on my tongue.

When I bend to kiss her, she smiles against my lips, and the thought of Indigo tasting herself makes me want to rip off her clothes and forget about this *taking it slow* thing.

"Fuck you," she whispers playfully, burying her head in the pillow.

"Soon," I chuckle as I wrap an arm around her and lead us toward the bathroom.

Indigo looks up at me, her big eyes watching me carefully. I lean down and kiss her deeply. She groans, threading her fingers through my hair, then gripping it tightly. She bites my lower lip, then breaks the kiss and snuggles her face into my neck.

With her still in my arms, I run the water in the tub.

"Do you want to wash your hair, too?" I ask.

She murmurs something, and when I look down, her mouth is parted, and her eyes are closed. I've never in my life seen a person fall half-asleep this fast, but it does something to me. I feel protective, responsible for her.

I continue to stay there, in the middle of the bathroom, with her in my arms for a couple more minutes, trying to convince myself this is actually happening. It feels strange to hold her, to do the things I've only imagined with her body, to have the freedom to kiss her, to wake up, and the first thing I see is her face.

Indigo has become every breath of air I take, every smile on my face, and every beat of my heart. She's become my every day.

While keeping one arm around her, I undress, then slowly slip her clothes off and throw them in the basket. She mumbles at every sudden move, but remains sleepy.

I lift her into the bathtub, being careful to not fall. I lower myself behind her so she's between my legs.

While I wash and massage her hair, she practically purrs with happiness, and my heart buzzes in my chest. It feels full and as much as I'd like to find a better explanation, I can't. I'm feeling at peace. Happy.

And I know now that no matter what happens between Indigo and I, I'll never be the same without her. I love to think that each experience takes us somewhere. I just hope this one will bring me the true love my mom always talks about.

After I realized that what I had with Ava was never love, I thought it would be impossible to have such intense feelings for someone. However, seeing Indigo this way, sleeping peacefully in my arms, makes my heart beat faster than it ever has. If she's the one, I won't be mad at the universe for it.

CHAPTER THIRTY FOUR
INDIGO

A SCREAM PIERCES THE NIGHT, making my heart beat so fast it almost flies out of my chest. I sit up, trying to adjust my eyes to the darkness. By the time my vision adapts, Elias is already at the bedroom door, tugging it open.

I follow him in a blur, hitting my head on the wall on my way there, my legs feeling wobbly. He goes right towards Olivia's room and my mind catches up.

Shit. Olivia. The screaming was hers.

This wakes me up like a bucket of ice water over my head. My mind can't keep up with the scenarios I start to imagine. Elias throws open the door with a loud thud and flicks the lights on.

I see his naked back relaxing as a relieved sigh escapes him. We enter the room and the tension in my shoulders eases when I see Olivia in bed.

He sits down next to her, and I lean over, brushing the hair off her sweaty forehead.

"It's okay," he whispers, taking her hand in his while

she continues to mumble in her sleep. "It's okay," he repeats, but something makes me think he's reassuring himself, and not her.

"She used to have a lot of nightmares when she was little." He keeps his voice low. "Especially after watching horror movies. She wasn't allowed, but she'd find a way to watch them anyway." Elias smiles at the memory and I don't stop caressing her. She scared the shit out of me.

"I still have some," I shrug, not really knowing why I say it.

He looks from his sister to me. "From watching horror movies?" he jokes, and I nod.

"Yeah. The only difference is that they were real."

A pained look crosses his features, like what I've said is nonsense, like I'm from a completely different world. I'm not. It's my reality.

"When did they stop?" he asks after leaning to kiss his sister on her head.

She's quiet now. Probably got rid of whatever monster was attacking her. I peck her forehead, and we leave her room. I answer him only after he clicks the door shut.

"After I started taking sleeping pills."

I'm sure he's noticed me taking them every night before bed.

He nods, swallowing. "Are you tired?"

"Not anymore," I smirk, and he mirrors it.

Goosebumps cover my skin at the memory of how we ended the night. It felt good to have him at my mercy. Never in my life have I felt this powerful. He was too much, and not enough, all at once.

He's different from the guys I've had before. There

weren't many. Just a couple, but neither of them made me climax. And Elias did it through clothes, in less than a minute.

And the other guys were... too basic. I lived with the idea that everyone exaggerated when it came to sexual experiences. Turns out they weren't and I like sex just fine.

He points his finger at the couch, and I sit on it. He makes himself a coffee, then sits next to me. The clock above the TV shows six thirty in the morning. There's no point in sleeping now. He would've got up for work in two hours anyway, and he'd wake me up with all the noise he makes. I swear he does it on purpose to make me a morning person.

"Can I ask what triggered them?" Elias says, grabbing my arm and laying me down so my head is on his legs. "The nightmares, I mean."

I stretch my legs and look him straight in the eyes. "My mom did a lot of shit to me and no one ever stopped her."

The information seems to satisfy him and I love him for not pushing me to tell more, but for the first time in my life, I feel like saying it out loud will free me of it.

"When I was a kid, I used to love her so much. I continued to do so, even when she'd slap me because of a bad grade at school or when she'd pull my hair because I dropped something," I laugh bitterly. "Then she'd use her shoe instead of her palm, and soon enough she'd replaced the shoe with a paddle."

"I'm so sorry, Indigo," he whispers, his hand playing with my hair.

I nod in agreement, knowing that Elias Madden doesn't say things just for the sake of it. He really means it.

I continue, "My father always looked away when he saw bruises on me. He had this saying: 'If your mother or I say it rains from the ground to the sky, then that's how it is.' That's all he ever said to me. So, I hid the marks with long jeans, even in the summer. Wouldn't have mattered even if I hadn't. I think I was seventeen, or close to it, when she took things too far. I was talking with this guy, Travis, and she told me to put the phone down. I didn't. She wanted to hit me again, and I was getting tired of it, so I got up and walked away from her. Long story short, she totally lost it. I tried to run upstairs and that somehow led to her banging my head on the floor until it bled."

Elias inhales sharply and stops stroking me.

"When I looked at myself in the mirror the next day, my eyes were purple, my lips bruised and my hair was stuck to my head with congealed blood. I snapped a picture, just in case." A resentful laugh escapes my lips again.

"How did you not just kill them in their sleep?" he asks, breathing heavily.

I feel his gaze on me, but I can no longer make eye contact. "I threatened them I'd go public; share the picture of me that morning and some texts from my mom."

"Did they buy it?"

"Not at first, no," I shake my head, "but they quickly learned not to underestimate me when a journalist knocked at the door, asking to see me for an interview."

"That was incredibly smart for a seventeen-year-old."

Normal people would appreciate that compliment. But not me. I *had* to be smart, and it's damn painful when you have to grow up so fast.

"So, they drew up a contract with a lawyer and shit. I'd

get my grandmother's house and fifty thousand a month, just to keep up the family appearance."

"And you agreed," he states, more for himself than me.

"Yes. Leaking everything wouldn't have got me anything in the long term, plus I was seventeen."

He nods, thinking deeply about it. It scares me when the silence extends for a minute or two. I start to worry about what he's going to say next. I care about him and his opinion.

"If you want to run, do it now," I joke, but not really. On the inside, I'm freaking out.

He's still quiet as I gather the courage to look at him. He has tears in his eyes. He's hurting for me. For her. For the girl that went through all that when all she wanted was to be a regular kid.

I reach up and wipe away a tear from the corner of his eye. And that tells me everything I need to know: he would never run away.

He keeps his gaze on me, not trying to hide his true feelings. I love that about him. I love many things about him. Many parts of him. And I'm afraid of the day when I'll love all of him.

CHAPTER THIRTY FIVE

ELIAS

"Who's that?" I ask when I hear the knock at the door.

Indigo shrugs, still on the phone with Cora. Apparently, she found a house that might be the perfect fit. They're setting up a viewing right now, and it makes me a little sad, knowing she'll leave soon. Having her around, especially in my bed, has become a great routine this week.

I open the door, revealing a delivery man. Frowning, I try to remember what I've ordered, but there's nothing I can think of.

"Good morning," the guy says, looking through the papers in his hand. "Can you sign here?" He hands me a pen and points to a page.

I take the pen from him. "For what, exactly?"

"It's a gift," he smiles cheerfully. "Sign this and we'll bring it over."

We? How big is this gift?

I do as asked and watch six guys carry a two-meter-long box into the house. I get out of their way, utterly confused about what's happening.

"Where do you want us to put it?" a guy with glasses asks as they enter.

"There?"

They put it down by the dining table.

"Thanks," I say with a raise of my hand, and close the door behind them.

I look for Indigo, but she's probably still on the phone somewhere, trying to find some peace and quiet. I can't blame her. She must be so stressed about finding a new home.

What she told me yesterday is still playing on my mind. I've never been aggressive, but all I could think of was beating the shit out of her parents and everyone that disrespected her.

I shake my head to clear my thoughts and bend to open the package. Indigo comes in just as the box walls fall, revealing a big gray couch, exactly like the one at her grandma's house.

"Eh?" She raises her arms in the air. "Much better, right?" Her smile is wide, and although I want to be mad at her for spending money on me, her joy is contagious.

I smile and nod. My current couch is so ugly and it's as hard as a plank. I remember telling her how much I loved the couch she had at her old place, and how comfortable it was, but that wasn't a hint for her to buy me one.

"But why?" I ask, embracing her and kissing the top of her head.

She takes a step back. "What do you mean? This was purely for selfish reasons."

I chuckle, and at this moment, it's like my entire

perception of her changes. My eyes see her differently. Something has shifted and I can't stop staring at her.

"I like you," I admit, and she cringes.

"No, you don't." She slaps my arm.

"I do," I push.

"Don't believe ya."

My hands grab her round ass, and I lift her up so she can wrap her legs around my torso. I step over what's left of the box and lower her onto the couch.

"Want me to prove it?" I ask, my hands squeezing her.

She shakes her head, but still pushes her hips toward me. "Nah, you only said it because I'm helping to get that ugly furniture out of your house."

I chuckle. "So creative, that pretty head of yours."

My lips trace kisses all over face, feeling her hot skin burning them away.

"Too..." she pushes me with her model hands, "many."

A lusty feeling of warmth steals over me, my fingers yearning to touch her, to feel her. Every inch of me lights up with the burning, urgent kisses I trace down her neck.

"You secretly love it," I say.

She swallows hard, proving how right I am. I slowly make my way lower, and then peel off her shorts and panties.

"I..." I slip a finger into her, "like..." another finger, "you." I lower my mouth to her, and tease her slowly, but firmly. "Just this much," I mumble, then swipe my tongue over her in one painfully leisurely move. Her hand grabs my hair.

"So damn sexy," I groan, enjoying her being in charge. I lower myself onto the couch next to her and pull her over me so she's straddling my torso. I look up into those incredible crystal eyes.

I pull her up my body so her wetness is inches from my face. I give her no time to register what's happening before I put my mouth on her again.

Indigo looks down at me and I'm lost. She starts riding me, her hands finding support on the couch cushions. I keep drawing circles with my tongue on her clit, deeply and hungrily. Guttural growls slip past my lips. Her entire body vibrates in response, the orgasm staring to crest like an ocean wave.

"Oh God," she shudders over me, arching her back.

This must be the best feeling on earth. She seems so free and I can't prevent my arousal from taking control, slipping my fingers into her again. And I don't stop, already leading her to the next climax.

And then the next one.

And the next.

CHAPTER THIRTY SIX
INDIGO

"AND THERE'S SOMETHING MORE," Elias says as I look around the big house. It's pretty similar to my grandma's, and at the same time, they look like they're from different worlds. The couch isn't that big, but at least it's prettier than the one Elias had. The kitchen is to the left, and it's missing a washing machine. Not a problem for me, but Enya might object. We'll figure something out.

The wooden stairs are rounded at the edges. They creak under every step, but I seem to find something oddly pleasing about that.

I turn to face Elias and Cora, and they both have devilish smiles on their faces.

"What?" I ask and place my hands on my hips.

"Come on," he says, beckoning me to the back door and I follow, eyeing him suspiciously.

To be honest, I'm already thinking about buying this place. The last few days were full of calls, and I hate calls. My patience is running out.

And this one here, this one has a lot of potential. Just a few little touch-ups and it's done.

"Indigo," Cora says, her hand on the doorknob, "meet your maybe-future garden."

I nod, trying to put my thoughts in place, to work out if I'm ready for this. It kind of feels overwhelming, knowing that I'm one step closer to replacing my grandma's garden with a new one. That's not something I want.

Just as Cora goes to open the door, a loud slam makes us all look behind.

"Wait!" Olivia yells. "Wait for me," she urges, bursting through the front door.

Elias laughs as she tries to catch her breath. She's wearing oversized pajamas composed of one of Tom's old T-shirts and a baggy pair of sweats.

"Fell—," she tries and shakes her head, "asleep."

Elias takes her in his arms, and she wraps her hands around him more tightly than I've ever seen before. He seems to notice too by the look on his face but says nothing. I'm sure he'll talk to her about it.

"How do you like the house?" Liv asks, releasing herself from the hug.

I shrug. "Let the garden decide whether I like it or not."

Liv nods and puts one of her hands on my back and the other on her brother's, a peaceful smile on her lips.

"What's up with you?" I whisper in her ear.

"It's just..." I hate how she flips it away like it's nothing. "Just love seeing the two of you together."

I give her a look. "We're not together. Not like that. I guess?" Don't know what to say. Feels weird. Elias and I definitely didn't talk about it, but we aren't just friends either.

"We could be?" he answers my question with a question. I want to rip his head off. The butterflies in my stomach say otherwise. They say I should kiss the shit out of him or something like that.

"Great," Olivia says, smiling up at both of us like it's all settled.

I shake my head, then nod at Cora for her to open the door. The sight that greets me takes my breath away.

"You didn't..." I say. My eyes start to water, and I try to blink them away. Hate to fucking cry in front of people. Elias nods, and I have the urge to punch him.

Or keep him forever.

That kind of scares me.

I walk forward tentatively. The garden is big. Much bigger than the one I had at home. *Home*, what a funny word. Your entire life you call a place home, and it turns out it's not forever. People say that as you age, your home is your safe place, and that place doesn't need to be physical. It can be a person. A book. Music.

I see it that way too.

Then I notice a tiny sapling. That makes me excited knowing I'm going to watch it grow. And there's plenty of space to plant more. As my grandmother loved to say, a gifted flower is never a waste.

I look at him, then at the tree. Then back again. From the corner of my eye, I see Cora taking a step back to give us privacy.

"Oh my God," I whisper and cover my face.

"What?" Elias asks, concern swimming in his voice.

"What happened?" Olivia pushes.

"The tree..."

"Yeah? What's with it?" Elias steps closer, putting a reassuring hand on my shoulder. "You don't like it?" He watches me in a way that makes me wish the world would swallow me up.

"What? No, of course I do," I admit. "I was talking about the little tree you planted at my grandma's. We left it there to die and replaced it like it was nothing."

The corners of his mouth rise in a relieved smile, and he touches his forehead to mine. He cradles my face in his hands and looks me straight in the eyes, his gaze going from one to the other like always.

"Hey," he puts on that breathtaking smile, "I'll plant you a damn forest if that's what you're worried about."

My knees go weak. I've never thought about getting on my knees for a man, but I'd drop in a second if he asked me to.

I don't know if I'm blushing or not, but the look in his eyes changes to a mischievous one. It's like he read my mind and is damn pleased about it.

"So," Olivia interrupts us, "are you buying it?"

We take our hands off each other, the tension suddenly too much. Especially the bit throbbing between my legs.

I clear my throat and turn toward Cora. She smiles before I even give her the answer.

"I am."

Elias suddenly sneaks his head between my legs from behind and stands up with me on his shoulders. His strong hands grip my ankles. He emits a loud *woohoo* and Olivia hugs us.

"I told you she has a good eye for old things." Cora points at Elias and he chuckles.

"Except for ugly old couches," I say and we all laugh, a light mood surrounding us.

I look down at him and the smile on my face won't stop growing.

Elias has been such a light in my life, bringing things into it I thought I'd never accept, getting me out of my comfort zone, and always being there for me. Things that no one else did for me.

He loves animals, his family, ketchup on his fried egg, brushing his curly hair in the morning, sleeping with a pillow between his legs, and my eyes. Don't know for sure about the last one, but no one's gaze has ever met mine the way his does.

He hates bright light in the morning, even though he's a morning person. He hates washing his hair, which is pretty odd since he loves washing mine.

I think I like him too.

CHAPTER THIRTY SEVEN
ELIAS

"So, are we... you know?" I ask.

We're driving to my parents' house. It's our first time going there since we became more than just friends, and I'd love to do it knowing our relationship is official. If that's what Indigo wants, of course.

"Depends." She shrugs, and I raise a brow.

"On what?"

I steal a glance at her. She's looking out the window, trying to hide a laugh. My hand squeezes her leg, and she gives me a playful look.

"Eyes on the road, bud, or you're never going to know the answer."

There's something about her mood today. She's doing good. A lot better compared to how she was just a couple of months back. She's lighter, eager to get out of her old routine, and she communicates a lot more. We're having fun together.

This version of her brings me comfort. I can't explain it.

It's just that I'm smiling a lot more lately. My heart feels happy and full.

"Will you help me with the garden?" she asks, and I laugh. That's the dumbest question she could ask.

I wish she'd give me a straight answer. She loves making me work for it and I'm starting to love it just as much. "Stop changing the subject and just say *yes* already," I laugh.

Indigo rolls her eyes, but there's still a smile on her face. "That's not the way to ask a woman to be your girlfriend." She fake pouts, crossing her arms over her chest.

I nod, agreeing with her. Both of us still smiling. I load up a song on the stereo by Dean Lewis. She listens to him every time she showers and I'm kind of a fan of his. She buries her head between her hands, groaning.

"Indigo—" I stop short. "Wait, what's your last name again?"

"Hayes," she laughs, her face still in her hands.

"Indigo Hayes, will you be my girlfriend?" I smile widely. She finally meets my gaze.

"I have to say yes, but only because you're nice company."

"Okay, girlfriend," I tease, knowing she won't like it.

She smacks me in the arm. "Don't say that."

"Don't say what?"

"Girlfriend." She waves her hand in the air. "It's weird. Don't make it weird."

"What do you mean?" I play dumb. "You just said it yourself."

She leans over without warning and gives me a fast peck on the lips.

"Great way to make a man shut his mouth," I chuckle.

"It worked though," she says as we arrive at my parents' house.

I shake my head, park the car, hop out and open the door for her. This feels like a big thing. Bringing home the first girl after Ava. Technically, it's not the first time, but my soul feels like it is.

"You look incredible," I say, sizing her up and licking my lips. It takes all my strength to stop from driving us back home and carrying her into bed.

While there's nothing different with her style of clothing, her attitude and what we've just settled changes it all.

"They already love you," I whisper in her ear as we enter the house. She relaxes a little as Mom, Dad, and Olivia give her a hug.

"Ahh!" Mom claps her hands together after hugging me. "You guys are thriving!"

"Is anyone in the mood for darts?" Dad asks and Mom slaps his arm playfully.

"Tom! Let them eat first."

"I'd love to," Indigo admits, and I nod beside her.

"But Lorelai's right. Let's eat first," Dad says.

We agree and eat at the fastest pace ever. Olivia doesn't eat much and when I ask her about it she says she ate some sweets a while ago and now her stomach hurts.

After we're all set, Indigo helps Mom wash the dishes, while Olivia, Dad, and I wait for them on the couch with full tummies. I can hardly move.

"We barely see you since you moved into town," Dad says, putting his hand on my shoulder.

"Yeah." He doesn't realize it, but that makes me feel

bad. I never want them to think that I don't want to visit. "Indigo keeps me busy," I say.

He laughs, understanding washing over his features. "I remember when I was like that with Lorelai." Dad smiles at the memory and Olivia cringes, probably having a flashback to the moment she caught us.

Can't blame her. I'd most likely throw up if I found Mom and Dad making out. I shudder, taking my mind off it.

"We'll visit more often," I promise. I'll have to see what Indigo thinks, but I'm pretty sure she'd love it. She's a sucker for Mom's cooking.

"Ready to go?" Mom asks from the kitchen door.

We decide to go in separate cars; Olivia, Indigo, and I in mine, and Mom and Dad in their ancient SUV.

"How's married life?" Olivia pokes Indigo from the back seat as we set off.

Indigo sighs, "I—"

"Oh my God! You should name your child Lucas if it's a boy and Avery if it's a girl." She claps excitedly.

I chuckle, "Too soon, kiddo."

Olivia pouts. "Promise me that's what you'll name them." She looks at me in the rearview mirror.

Indigo shakes her head. "What? No," she laughs and Liv taps her head playfully.

"Why not? I named Mushroom, remember? It would only be fair to do the same with your kids."

"Yeah, but that's—"

"He genuinely looked like one."

Indigo sighs and gives up. "You'll forget by the time I have babies."

Olivia growls, "Say yes."

"No."

"E?" Olivia turns to me, waiting for me to defend her.

"Oh no." I shake my head. "I'm deaf when it comes to you two arguing."

"Please?"

She's giving us those puppy dog eyes in the mirror. They're impossible to resist.

Indigo sighs. "Okay, yes."

Olivia throws her arms around Indigo from behind, squeezing her.

I'm not ready for babies, but if it involves Indigo, it might not be that bad when the time comes.

CHAPTER THIRTY EIGHT
INDIGO

"I'm gonna take a shower," I groan and get out of bed, stretching awkwardly. "My back hurts from all the games I won."

"Dad let you," Elias jokes, looking up at me. He's stretched out on the bed, arms beneath his head. No shirt on.

Rolling my eyes, I pick my clothes out for the day. "We both know your dad is too proud to let anyone win."

Elias chuckles. He knows that better than I do. Lorelai told me his dad has never, not even once, let Elias or Olivia win. He'd get bitter and grumpy if he wasn't leading the game.

We all have our flaws. It's actually pretty funny. He pouted like a child when I won — by a huge margin — and I couldn't help but laugh. Olivia squealed with delight, and came to hug me, happy that someone had finally defeated her dad.

I enter the bathroom and leave the door ajar. He'll come

in sooner or later, and the thought makes me nervous, even though it's my choice to leave the door open.

Last night, I kept picturing getting on my knees for him. Dreamed about it. Woke up with my panties soaked and more turned on than ever. I'm not sure how good I'd be at it since I've never done it for a man, but I want to do it for him. And that thought alone makes me squeeze my thighs together.

I open the shower and step in, the water playing over my naked body. For a couple of minutes, I just stand there, contemplating everything that's happened lately.

Baby steps are hard to do in real life. If you want life to go slowly, it only seems to speed up. My process with Elias has been tough *and* fast. That doesn't mean I'm fully healed; it just means I don't have to work as hard on it as I used to.

It feels like I'm living a dream, in a bubble that could pop at any time. I'd say this moment won't last forever, but having faith in a positive future won't harm me. Hopefully.

If I think about it, even leaving my mom's grasp was a good thing. I needed change and closure. That's what the new house is giving me. A lot of things have changed, but at the same time, they're like they've always been. Enya still works for me — actually, what she's doing is more than work — and Olivia still makes my head hurt. I think I'll probably even start walking dogs again.

Warm hands massage my shoulders, shaking me from my thoughts, slipping a soft moan from me.

"I'm hard from that alone," Elias teases, kissing my back.

I turn around; I want to see him. I can't get enough of looking at him lately.

He's so different inside and outside the bedroom. Elias is a respectful guy, and he might seem innocent at first, but once he gets you in bed, it's game over. So forceful and rough. Can't say that I don't like it. In fact, it only makes me greedier.

And I like to think he's that way because of me. Because he's hungry for me, just as much as I am for him. I can't stop picturing him naked. It's almost outrageous how much I crave him.

"I love your eyes so much," he whispers, looking deeply into them while brushing his thumb over my bottom lip. "Your hair too." He smiles, whirling a strand of it between his fingers.

I believe him. He'd never lie.

An image of me on my knees, gazing up at him with those eyes he loves so much, comes to mind. I slowly start to lower myself.

"Whoa, whoa," he says, grabbing my arms to stop me from going further. He grins at me and smooths my cheek with his thumb, his strong fingers cradling the back of my head like a warm blanket.

My eyes almost close at the sensation. He feels so good. So comfortable.

"You don't have to do it," he says.

But what he doesn't say is that he wants me to. I can see it in his eyes and that makes me want to do it even more.

"Didn't you say that you love my eyes?" I whisper, moving one inch lower, pinning him with my gaze.

"Yeah, but—"

The rest doesn't matter to me. I drop to my knees.

I grab his length with my hand while I use my tongue to encircle the tip. He's big. Even though I can't swallow him whole, my hand and mouth succeed in covering him almost entirely.

"Oh shit," he flinches, running his fingers through my hair, then grasping it tightly.

I gaze up at him. He looks drunk. Can't keep his eyelids open. Doing his best to stay upright.

"How do you like my eyes now?" I tease, taking him out of my mouth only to plunge him back in.

He lets out a masculine growl and my core tightens. One of my fingers slides down between my legs and I gently massage myself while I please him. Who knew that giving pleasure to someone else would be this enjoyable?

"Tell me, how much do you like them?" I ask again.

"You'll learn in a bit how much."

His voice is different. Harsh. The fucking victory I feel knowing I'm the one that makes him feel this way is incredible.

And I want to give him more. I keep working my tongue while I move my mouth up and down his shaft.

His phone rings from the bedroom. He ignores it.

I'm glad about that. Glad I can hold his attention. He tilts his face up to the ceiling, his eyes closed, regular moans escaping his mouth. His phone rings again. Elias ignores it again, keeping his hand on my head as I pick up the pace.

He's close to finishing. As his legs start to shudder, I take him out of my mouth but keep working his length. He reaches down and palms my breasts, squeezing them, relishing them. It's my turn to shudder as the pressure between my legs builds. We lock eyes and he moans, spilling his warm seed all over my breasts. The sight of it tips me over the edge and I come too, shuddering and squirming from pleasure.

"That was so damn hot," he says. He pulls me up and kisses me deeply, not caring that he was in my mouth just moments ago.

He presses his forehead to mine, slowing his breath, then runs the shower head over me, soaping and cleaning every inch of me.

Elias is taking his time; this is no longer anything sexual. He's caressing every part of me, treating it like it's made of glass.

I thought touching would never be a love language for me, but his touches spread warmth all over my body, no matter if it's a tap on the shoulder or a gentle squeeze of my thigh.

"I want to take art classes," I say suddenly. It's something I've thought about a few times lately. It's out of nowhere, but I want him to know. It's a big step toward achieving my goal of doing something with my own talent. I'm pretty good at it and it gives me a dream to chase. Just like Elias.

He smiles down at me. "I think that'd be good. Maybe you could teach others one day, too?"

The suggestion warms my insides. I gaze up at him. I'm loving the idea of helping others on a road that was difficult for me to walk. Drawing is challenging, like anything else you love to do, because when you love something, you put your whole heart into it. If it starts to feel like that isn't enough, you quit.

I'd love to look at art therapy in the future, too. People could learn techniques for drawing and painting, and at the same time, work on themselves.

Excitement lights up my features, and Elias nods, a grin taking over his beautiful full lips.

"I'd love that," I confess.

He lowers and brushes his mouth over mine, making me quiver at the sweet tenderness of his kiss. His phone rings again. We break apart and he groans.

"I'll be right back." Elias gives my cheek a peck before stepping out of the shower to grab it.

"It's Dad," he announces before answering, and puts him on speakerphone as he dresses. "Hi Dad, what's up?"

I turn off the shower, grab a towel, and join him in the bedroom. I can hear his Mom crying in the background and Tom is sobbing quietly.

My brain feels waterlogged, clouds and murky thoughts taking over. What the hell is going on?

"What happened?" Elias asks when Tom doesn't say anything.

"You should come home," he sighs. "It's Olivia." When his dad says her name, Lorelai starts crying even harder, the sound ripping me in two.

I've never in my life heard a more painful thing. Elias looks at me, shock glistening in his eyes. He tells his dad he'll be there in a few minutes and hangs up.

I dry myself as he dresses. I stay silent. He's barely there, his stare broken. Empty.

"I—," he says, pointing at the door after throwing a shirt on, "I'm gonna go." He doesn't even look at me, his hand shaking as he raises it to his mouth.

"I'm coming with you," I say, throwing some sweats and a jumper on. My voice is calm and reassuring. The opposite of how I actually feel.

He nods, grabs his keys from the nightstand and rushes to the door. I run after him, feeling like I might throw up at any moment. Was it a car accident? Did she fall or something?

"Are they home?" I ask. If my fears are right, she's probably in a hospital.

Elias nods, although I don't think he's aware of what he's doing. When I see him go for the driver's door I grab his shoulder.

"Let me," I say. He nods again and gives me the keys.

I drive as fast as I can. Elias just stares out of the window, jiggling his leg. I want to say it's going to be okay, but he's never lied to me and I won't either. I can't reassure him about something I know nothing about.

"We'll figure it out." That's the only thing I say. It's the closest to the truth, despite whatever awaits us.

CHAPTER THIRTY-NINE
ELIAS

I KEEP TELLING myself it's not real. Saying it over and over until it's enough to make me believe it. But no matter how many times I say it, I'm shaking as the fearful images build in my mind. Just thinking of it shatters me, tears me apart. There's a question that roughly stabs at my heart.

I see the ambulance as soon as we approach the house, and I leap out of the car as it's still moving. Indigo screams something at me, but I can't hear it. My feet fly as I cross the distance to the house. My heart is beating like it might stop at any second and I gasp for breath. Not from the run, but from the sight before me: my sister's lifeless body on a gurney, my parents shuffling after the paramedics.

Mom falls to her knees, tears streaming down her face, eyes red. Dad caresses her. When he realizes I'm standing there, frozen, he looks up at me and I feel my heart break.

Never in my life have I seen my father crying and it rips me to pieces. I can't explain how it feels to hold your dad as he shakes with sobs. It makes my stomach twist and I cover my mouth to stop from throwing up.

"Don't take her," Mom screams at one of the men.

They don't listen, continuing to walk toward the ambulance. Mom grabs one of them by the shirt, weeping with grief.

"She's my daughter," she says, crying even harder. The man starts to walk again.

The sounds she's making are too hard to take in. I feel weak and nauseous. Can't really think. Or see. My vision is blurred. All I can do is replay images of my sister hugging me tightly. Was I blind not to notice that something was wrong? She wasn't eating as much as usual, her attitude had changed. I was stupid to think it was just a teenage thing. Something must've been wrong.

"Don't you have a fucking soul?" I hear Indigo shout and I look for her. "Let them say their goodbyes," she says through gritted teeth, standing beside my sister. The men finally nod.

Mom and Dad go to her, but I can't move. My feet are glued to the ground and my eyes to her tiny body. She shouldn't be there. She's supposed to grow, graduate high school, find a boyfriend, make cakes with Mom, sleep in her room at my place whenever she wants to.

What's she doing there? Eyes closed. Not moving. Not saying a word. That's not her. That's not my Olivia. Olivia would never walk past without a hug. My sister would never stop talking. Can't she see how much she's hurting us? Why won't she wake up?

"Elias," says Indigo. I feel a warm hand on my shoulder and I flinch, taken by surprise. "Come." I don't ask where, I just robotically follow her as she grabs my hand and leads me to Olivia.

Seeing her this close only proves my point. This is not my sister. There's no smile on her face. No lecture on her lips. No sign that she was once happy.

Olivia is still as beautiful as ever, but her beauty seems empty.

"My baby," my mom cries on her chest, and until Indigo takes me in her embrace, I don't even realize I'm crying too.

"What happened?" I ask. My voice sounds distant. Unrecognizable.

Mom searches her pockets and hands me four white envelopes. One says 'Mom and Dad', another is for me, one is for Indigo, and the last one, written in her neat writing, says 'For the world'.

"I—" Mom starts, but a cry of pain interrupts her, "I couldn't—"

"Shhh." Dad takes her in his arms, kissing the top of her head as tears drop from his chin to her hair.

I look at the envelopes in my hands and then at my parents.

"She...?"

Mom starts crying even harder, leaning over and kissing her daughter's cheek, but doesn't answer me. Dad just nods his head.

I hear Indigo gasp. She quickly pushes me aside and vomits onto the front lawn.

"It's okay," Mom says, wiping her nose. "She's going to wake up. Did you hear me, baby? You have to wake up, okay?" She shakes Olivia's body and Dad gently takes her aside. He nods to the paramedics to take my sister.

"Tom!" Mom screams. "I'll never forgive you!" She beats at his chest. "Don't let them take her!"

Dad continues to cry silently and tries to guide her to their car.

"Thomas, please don't do this to me. Please don't do this to me." She takes his face in her hands, trying to get him to look at her.

"Lorelai," he whispers, his voice breaking, "we have to let her go."

Dad puts a reassuring hand on her cheek, but she smacks it away. And that breaks Dad apart. He just cries soundlessly as she continues to howl.

"Take me back to her," she pushes him. "She's my daughter!"

"She's my daughter too!" he wails and Mom freezes, then falls into his arms.

I watch as the paramedics take my sister, close the ambulance door, and drive away, leaving a broken family behind.

"See you at the hospital," Dad says in a weak and tremulous whisper, sending frightened anticipation down my spine. Indigo takes my hand, puts me in the car, clips in my seatbelt, closes the door, and drives us away.

I stare at the envelopes in my hands, deciding whether I should open my letter or not. Seems risky. Too soon.

But I want to know why she did it. Maybe she thought we didn't love her anymore? Were her school grades bad? Were the other kids bullying her?

I sigh and open the envelope. As soon as I see her handwriting, my eyes blur with tears and I need a minute to clear my vision before I can read it.

. . .

DEAR ELIAS,

If you're reading this, it means I've found the courage to do it.

Please don't be mad at me or yourself. You had nothing to do with this. You were nothing but a good brother, my biggest supporter, and my greatest friend. I want you to know that I've always loved you very much and I still love you now.

I would've loved to see you marry and have kids (preferably with Indigo — I really think she's the one). And I will. I know I will. It's just that I'll be looking from above.

Know that every time you see a butterfly, it's me saying 'I love you'. When Avocado barks at the door and no one is there, just know it was me. With every beat of your heart, I'm right beside you.

You must believe me when I say there's no easy way to do this. Say goodbye I mean. I know you're all hurting, but would you believe me if I told you that I'm better off here? Please do. Don't ever stop smiling. With every smile, I'm closer to you. With every tear, I'm further away.

Take care of Mom and Dad. Help them get through this. I know Indigo will help them too. They love her like their own child and they barely know her.

And remember what we spoke about? Yesterday? Yeah, kid's names. Brother, I know you're mad at me, but you can't imagine how bad I'm going to haunt you if you don't respect my wish.

I just hope I won't catch you and Indigo... you know. I've erased that from my memory, and I don't need a redo, thanks.

Please read the 'For the world' letter at my funeral. That will answer all your questions.

I love you, big bro. I'll miss you and I know you'll miss me too, but I'm begging you, don't let that ruin your life. Make tree therapy a real thing, make Indigo happy, put a ring on her finger, and save me a chair at your wedding.

Livy x

CHAPTER FORTY
INDIGO

I HATE FUNERALS.

They only bring back black memories. Moments that no one should have to go through. It's like an out-of-body experience. You see everyone, hear everyone, but you're trapped inside. Numb.

Can't even imagine how Elias is feeling. I once heard that sibling relationships are tangled in a way no other can be. He must be in so much pain.

His mom is silent. I guess that's not good compared to how she was only a few days ago. She might've read her letter.

Elias has been pretty silent too. Smiling when he sees me wake up, but only for a second. After that, the smile disappears like he's not allowed to feel any joy.

I feel that way too. There aren't many reasons to smile, anyway. Just him.

We're all in a private tiny room at the back of the chapel, with a couple of boxes of bottled water and three chairs. I'm the one standing up because it felt like the right thing to do. They're suffering the most.

I'm not saying I'm not suffering — I can't even feel my legs anymore — but I can stand and that's enough.

Lorelai looks utterly defeated, all dressed in black for her daughter's funeral. Tom's just there for her, a hand in her hair, kissing the top of her head from time to time, looking empty.

Lorelai clears her throat. "I can't read the letter," her voice breaks, and Elias's dad nods.

"I'll do it," he says, before Elias has time to offer.

Tom takes the letter from Lorelai and opens it, a sigh escaping him as he sees her writing. He traces his fingers over it, tears filling his eyes.

I grab Elias's hand. I give it a squeeze, trying my best to be there for him, although I don't know how to do it for myself.

"Hi," Tom says, reading the letter, his voice already cracking, "I clearly don't know how to start this. I've never had to do this and I'd wished I'd never have to, but if you're reading this... I'm sorry. I love all of you, Indigo included. I know she's there and I don't want her to feel left out."

His dad smiles just a tiny bit, and I do too, hearing her voice through the words.

"Me doing this has nothing to do with any of you. Life was good until two months ago when a part of me stopped living. Guess that's an understatement. The only moments I'd feel alive were around each of you."

Lorelai sniffles, fighting back a sob, while Elias squeezes my hand. I don't know if he realizes he's doing it. Don't really mind. He can break it for all I care.

Tom continues, "I don't remember the date, which might be weird for you because victims normally remember it, apparently. Well, not me. I remember fragments of it. How I got out of class and took a shortcut home. That was my life-changing mistake. There's no easy way to say this, but I want you to know the truth. I was—" he stops, sucking in a deep breath before raising a shaky hand to his mouth.

His face turns white, his hand closes into a fist and he presses it into his mouth, his whole body shaking.

Fuck. It's that bad.

"I was raped—," he stops again, cursing under his breath, trying to get through this torture, "by my school counsellor. I was disgusted with myself. His touch was everywhere, no matter how much I tried to wash it off."

Elias stands up, unsteady on his feet. I feel sick to my stomach and cover my mouth with a hand, afraid I might throw up.

"I don't hate him any more than I hate myself for what happened. I pray that you never have to feel your body broken while your mind watches from afar." Tom breaks down in sobs.

Lorelai is still silent. Don't know what to do. I want to go and comfort her, but I don't know how to do it or *if* I should do it. The only thing she wants is her daughter back.

"Jesus Christ, Livy," Tom whispers, tears falling from his face to the paper shaking in his grasp. He continues to read, "Please understand that I've never gotten over this. Don't waste your life trying to make things right. Grieve, cry, but this is the last day. Continue with life because I'm still there. As I've said to each one of you: With every smile, I'm closer to you. With every tear, I'm further away."

Lorelai nods, listening carefully to the words, staring at the ceiling, hands tangled in her lap.

"When your heart beats, know that I'm there. With love, Olivia."

We all burst out crying, each shake of our body bringing us closer together. Their sobs mix with mine, making us one. We share the pain with each touch, not making it feel better, but understanding it, flowing into it.

None of us speak, not until our eyes are red, our throats burn and the tears dry on our faces.

"I knew something was off with her," Lorelai confesses, wiping her nose with a tissue. "I thought she liked a boy and was weird about it."

Her mouth twitches and I can't stop from saying, "It wasn't your fault, Lorelai."

She shakes her head. "But it was. I'm her mother. I should've known."

"You were only giving her space and not many mothers can do that." I hug her and she shudders in my embrace.

"I feel like I've failed her," she admits.

"Not you," I whisper. "The world has failed the smartest, funniest, and most beautiful girl. You raised her in the best way possible."

I feel Elias touching my back, comforting me while I comfort his mother. His father hugs him and all four of us cry again before going out into the churchyard.

Seeing her lowered into the ground feels wrong. Like she's being buried alive. This can't be real. But it is, and the only thing I find comfort in is that someone I know waits for her up there.

"My grandma will take good care of her," I whisper and Elias nods, kissing the top of my head, shaking with sobs.

CHAPTER FORTY ONE
INDIGO

I'm NOT ready to open my eyes or move my body.

I woke up an hour ago and I just can't stop replaying everything. How selfish I was not to notice. How she hugged us like it was the last time. How she insisted on names for our future kids. We were all too blind to see it.

She must've felt so alone. Not talking to someone does that to you.

Skipped therapy this morning. Darla has probably spammed me with texts, but I don't feel like explaining what's happened in the last few days.

Images of Olivia's body as it was lowered into the ground flash through my mind. Then I remember how it was with my grandma. The images blur into one. They cause me the same pain.

This is how I felt when my grandma died. No courage to wake up, choosing to stay in bed all day. I don't want to be that person again. And it's my job to not let Elias fall into a deep black hole, at the risk of never getting him out.

I sigh, open my eyes, and look at the ceiling. I turn

around to hug Elias, only to find a cold and lonely bed. He always wakes up before me, but he never gets up until I do.

Massaging my temples, I get out of bed and look for him. He can't have gone far. My heart starts to race and I find I can't breathe properly. He'll give me a damn heart attack.

I search for him everywhere: Olivia's room, the kitchen, the bathroom, the garden. He's nowhere to be found.

As I grab my phone from the nightstand, it lights up with a message from him. I sit down and open the text. There are a few others from my therapist, but I'll ignore them for now.

———

Saturday, 8 AM

Elias: I'm leaving for a few days
Elias: I'll be back before you know it
Elias: Take good care of Avocado for me and the house xx

Indigo: You can come back
Indigo: So sorry for invading your space

Elias: Stay
Elias: I just need to clear my head a little
Elias: Please be there when I come back?

Indigo: Just come home when you're ready

I DON'T REPLY to his last text. Not because I'm mad, but because I don't know what to say anymore. Can't think of anything that would change his mind and I don't want to either. He's an adult and I respect his decision.

The phone stays glued in my grasp for a while, my gaze lingering on the wall.

It's not hard to understand why he left. Things got too much, too overwhelming. He couldn't keep up anymore. Everyone and everything must remind him of her. Can't blame him for wanting some time alone.

I was in his place once, so that's maybe why I'm not mad at him. When my grandma died, I used to feel her presence everywhere. It might sound stupid, but I wanted to get rid of it. It was morbid and painful, but then one night I dreamed about her.

It was a beautiful dream. I was crying rivers and she came to me and put a hand on my cheek, watching me with mercy. We didn't say a word. Only exchanged caring glances and touches of understanding.

I regret rejecting her even now. I was stupid to run away from the only thing that would've stopped my grief.

Leaving home was just a defense mechanism that only made me sink further into agony. It's only now, after three years, that I realize trying to escape from things will never put an end to them. You must face them no matter what.

So, yes. I understand why he's doing this, and I know what a mess he is now. I just wish I could be there to comfort him, but again, I was the same and never accepted anyone's help. That doesn't mean it wasn't needed.

The thing is that I never came back and I'm afraid he

might not either. And that scares me more than I'd like to admit.

I've grown attached to him and knowing how hard I worked to let him into my life will make letting him go even harder. Elias is not someone I should let walk away. But I have no right to stop him. He needs to do things on his own.

Even though there's a chance he won't come back, I'd still be at peace with it if it helped him get through this grief. Although, that's not possible, anyway. You never truly get over losing someone you love.

You just get used to it. Their smell fades after a couple of months. After a year you can't hear their laugh anymore. And soon enough, their features aren't as clear as they once were.

Of course, you don't forget them, but the memory will never be as strong as having them there with you. And that hurts. It hurts so much that you only visit their grave when something important happens in your life. Not even when it's their birthday, because it's painful not to have them celebrating it with you.

And the hardest thing is that it's never going to be the same without them.

CHAPTER FORTY TWO

ELIAS

NEVER IN MY life have I imagined it would be this hard to leave a girl. Indigo is not just a girl, she's the woman my sister chose for me, she's the one whose smile lights up a room.

My plan was to wake up and have a chat with her about how I'm feeling. I failed at that. By a long way. I just couldn't bear to tell her I'm leaving when all I want to do is stay in her arms. Leaving isn't something I want to do, it's something I *need* to do.

So, instead of being an adult and telling her my plans, I decided to be a prick and just message her. I hope she doesn't see this as a breakup.

It's not.

I'm not separating myself from her. It's just that right now, even she reminds me of Olivia. I know that in the future that will warm my heart, but right now it only hurts.

Everything smells like Liv. The house, my clothes, the air.

Would she still do it if she knew how much it would affect me? If she knew it would tear my heart to shreds?

I've spent the past two days on the road, sleeping at shitty motels, memorizing every word she wrote. Olivia wanted me to stop thinking. But I can't. This escape will give me time to let everything sink in. And only after that will I start trying to make her wish come true.

As I enter a diner, Dad calls. I know hanging up isn't the right thing to do, but I'm not in the mood to talk, so I shoot him a text to let him know I'm out of town.

I sit at a table in the corner and take my laptop out, order a latte macchiato, and start putting all my tree therapy research into one place, preparing a portfolio.

Some well-known botanists reached out to me and asked me to make a portfolio to present to them. If everything goes well, we can make tree therapy a real thing by the end of this year.

That's how fast things happen when people like Henry Evans and Vanessa Scott get involved. I'll do my best to not let them down.

I have two weeks until I meet them and I'm going to work on it every day.

"Here you go," the waiter says kindly, and I thank him with a lazy smile. "Is there anything else I can do for you?"

I shake my head. "Nah, I'm good, thanks."

He nods and walks back to the kitchen. I take a sip. This is the best coffee I've ever drunk and I'll need more if I'm going to spend the day here, plotting my presentation.

I'll head back to my motel to sleep at some point. I'll need to get some rest for tomorrow morning as I'm leaving for the next town. By then, I should be able to get a good chunk of the presentation done.

And that's exactly what happens. I write, edit, rewrite, and think better about it. The hours pass in the blink of an eye.

CHAPTER FORTY THREE
INDIGO

IT'S BEEN a week since Elias left and I'm trying not to ask him what 'a few days' means. He could be home today for all I know. Or in a couple of weeks.

I'm staying on his new couch, Dog One on my lap and Dog Two on the carpet, while Avocado sleeps in Elias's bed. His bed is comfortable. It's just that it's not the same when I'm alone.

Yesterday, I almost grabbed the dogs and went home, but then I remembered he asked me to be here when he gets back. And I will.

The thing is, I'm not coping very well. The shock of Olivia dying was like falling from a cliff and surviving, only to breathe in a paralyzed body. And when Elias left, he took my last breath with him.

My phone rings, shaking me from my thoughts. It can't be Elias because we spoke a couple of hours ago and he only rings once a day.

'Darla The Therapist' shows on my screen. I sigh and hit the green button. "What?"

She lets out a relieved breath. "Jesus, Indigo. I thought you were dead."

I know that's a thing people say as a joke, but it only reminds me of Olivia's lifeless body. Not that I've stopped thinking about her anyway. Every thought I have is about her or her brother. It's overwhelming and tiring. It never stops. Not even in my sleep.

"Well," I say, "not me." A bitter laugh escapes me as my eyes fill with tears.

Darla falls silent for a moment, contemplating my words. "What do you mean?" she finally says. I can hear the trepidation in her voice.

I shrug and my lip quivers. My breath hitches and I let out a shaking sob as tears stream from my eyes.

"What happened?" she asks calmly, lowering her tone.

I don't say a word. I can't stop my emotions as they burst out. They feel like a fucking queasy carousel mixed with a tornado and my chest explodes with pain.

Darla stays on the line, waiting patiently, not pressing me to say anything. Maybe because she knows I'd hang up. Or because she's good at her job.

Dog One sits up on my belly and gives my nose a lick. I pat him on the head and a sad chuckle reverberates through my body. "Good boy," I whisper, sniffing.

"Do you want to talk about it?"

I contemplate her question. Do I want to talk about it? No. Do I need to? Probably. She told me once that holding in emotions would bring me more pain than letting them out. And I believe her. "Yeah," I sigh.

I tell her everything, not missing a single detail. I guess deep down I was eager to tell someone about it. Each word out of my mouth takes with it a stone from my heart. Breathing suddenly feels a lot easier.

She doesn't interrupt me or make comments. Darla lets me cry, take breaks when I don't feel like I can talk anymore, waits for me, and listens patiently. She doesn't say she's sorry, the thing people often say at times like this. She's quiet.

"And I haven't even opened the letter yet," I confess, and she sucks in a breath.

"I think you should. There's a big chance it'll make you feel closer to her."

I nod and stare up at the ceiling.

"You might be thinking that you were on the right path and Olivia's death took that from you, but you're still on it, Indigo. As long as you don't slip, you'll be fine."

"How can I make sure I don't slip?"

"Find something to keep you steady."

"Like what?"

"Little things. Take care of the garden, read the letter, paint, or start running. Anything that could help take your mind off things."

"Yeah," I agree, thinking about how I've spent the last week.

All I did was wake up, cry, eat, watch some movies, cry some more, and then sleep. Seems pathetic. That's not what I want from my life. I didn't take a step forward, only to take a thousand more back.

"And I expect to see you tomorrow," she says in a mothering tone, almost making me laugh.

I hang up and look at the white envelope on the table that bears my name. It's been there since she died. Elias read his. Took it with him. We all heard his father reading the one dedicated to all of us, but the courage to read mine never came.

Fuck it.

I snatch it up and rip it open, careful not to damage the paper inside. I unfold the letter and shiver when I see her neat writing.

Hi Blue!

Met your grandma up here. She's pretty cool. She braids my hair and tells me stories about you. She's even shown me your baby pictures. She wants you to know that she has her own garden with Mushroom in it and that she takes good care of him. Now I'll take care of her, too.

I'm good here. Happy. No intrusive thoughts, no sadness. Everyone here is content.

My biggest wish is for you guys to have peace and I won't find mine fully until that happens. I know it was selfish for me to do it and I'm sorry you feel how you feel right now, but if there was something that could've helped me, I promise I would've stayed. No therapy could erase those moments. They were on repeat for two whole months.

In my mind, I never got away, Blue. Do you know how it feels to be stuck in your own mind? In your own memories. I wanted out. I wanted to end it.

So I did. And it feels good. Like a fresh start.

You have to see it the way I do. You wouldn't want me to be sad, right? Then don't be. Think about how this released me from the pain I was in. I love you. I know I never got the chance to tell you, but I do. You were my only friend, and as grumpy as you were to start with, you turned into this beautiful woman. A woman that has the courage to say out loud that she has a problem and she's ready to face it.

You just said 'fuck it', Blue (Mom would've totally shouted 'language!'). You crawled out of the dark, and even though you fought demons at every turn, you still kept going.

I'm so proud of you. Don't let what happened take you down again. I don't want to be the reason you went back. You're strong enough to resist. I just know it. You did it once. Now all you have to do is stay, and that is a lot easier.

Please take care of Elias. I see the way he looks at you. I even see the way you look at him when you think he won't notice. He's the one, Indigo. Stop doubting it. Stop asking yourself if it's going to work. It is! I'm up here, doing my best to protect your relationship. You just have to be ready to fight for it.

He loves you. I'm pretty sure he doesn't know it yet, and something tells me you don't know your feelings either, but it won't be long until you both realize it.

And keep this in mind: With every smile, I'm closer to you. With every tear, I'm further away.

If you think I'm gone or no longer next to you, know that every time you see a butterfly it's me saying 'I love you'. When your dogs bark at nothing, just know it was me. With every beat of your heart, I'm right beside you.

Don't forget: If it's a girl, Avery. If it's a boy, Lucas. Got it?

Livy x

. . .

I DROP the tear-stained letter and cover my burning face with my hands. It hurts how smart she was. How she anticipated everything. How she knew the right things to say.

Knowing my grandma and her might be in heaven together calms my heart in an inexplicable way. It brings me peace.

Thinking her brother might love me also brings comfort. I know I have feelings for him, it's just that I've never put a label on them.

I just hope his love for me will be enough to bring him back home.

Sunday, 10:20 AM

Indigo: I just finished reading it.

Elias: The letter?

Indigo: Yeah

Elias: Are you okay?

Indigo: Not really

Elias: Want to talk about it?

Indigo: How are you?
Indigo: Better?

Elias: Message received
Elias: I'll call you in a bit

Indigo: Okay

Monday, 4:01 AM

Elias: Had a dream about her

Indigo: Are you okay?

Elias: Why are you awake?
Elias: It's 4 AM

Indigo: Can't sleep

Elias: Go to sleep. We'll talk tomorrow

Indigo: Want me to call you?

Elias: Yeah

Tuesday, 3:21 PM

Indigo: Avocado peed all over the couch

Elias: Really??
Elias: That's not like him

Indigo: And guess what?

Elias: What?

Indigo: I was on the couch
Indigo: Sleeping.

Elias: =)))

Indigo: Do you think that's funny?
Indigo: Remember there are three dogs in the house
Indigo: Their shit is going on your side of the bed

Wednesday, 1:46 AM

Indigo: It sucks

Elias: What?

Indigo: That I miss you

Elias: I miss you too
Elias: a LOT

Indigo: Yea

Elias: Don't be like that
Elias: I do

Indigo: Right.

Elias: I promise I'm not staying much longer
Elias: Indigo?

Thursday, 3:09 PM

Elias: I'm sorry.

Elias: I really miss you and it fucks with my head

Elias: I'll be home before Monday, okay?

Elias: And then I'm never leaving you again

Indigo: I'm sorry too.

Elias: For what?

Indigo: Because I got caught up in my feelings

Elias: It's okay, you have every right to be mad at me

Indigo: I'm not mad you

Friday, 9:21 AM

Indigo: Your sister said in her letter that you love me

Elias: She did?

Indigo: Yeah.
Indigo: Said the same thing about me

Elias: And you do?

CHAPTER FORTY FOUR
INDIGO

BREAD WITH WATER and sugar has been the only thing that's kept me alive for the past fourteen days. And pizza. I hate to cook. Enya had promised to prepare something for me, but I talked her out of it and told her to stay with the kids at my house for a few days instead.

She's not very happy with how I cope. I'm not fully proud of myself either, but it's better than never getting out of bed again.

I just got home from a run and Darla's name was on my lips the whole time. Can't remember the last time I ran or the last time I walked more than the distance from my front porch to my car. Maybe high school?

The thing is, I really enjoyed it. It was something close to therapy for my body, but now my legs are shaking badly.

At first, it felt amazing. Refreshing almost. Then my legs started to hurt a bit and I thought I'd just run a little more. Here's the thing: I forgot that I also have to run back.

Imagine a sweaty me, stopping on a bench for a quick rest, smiling proudly at myself because I ran so much, and then remembering I have to go all the way back again. Thought about calling a taxi. Then Darla appeared in my mind, shaking her head at me.

Well, thanks to you Darla, I can barely walk and my stomach is screaming with hunger. Not even my grandma's sugar-bread recipe makes it better.

I grab my phone from the table, food in my mouth, and open my chat with Elias. We've spoken every day through text or calls. Didn't feel like he was distant, just hurt. The only thing I regret is snapping at him in a moment of weakness.

And how our last conversation ended. He asked me if Olivia was right about loving him and I panicked. That's not how I wanted it to go. I texted him to ask about his feelings, but when he asked about mine, I got scared.

I haven't responded yet. Neither has he. I know I'm the one that should send him a message, and I will, but not right at this time. I don't even know what to say to him. He knows me by now, that's for sure. However, that's not going to help him read my mind.

A sigh slips from my mouth as I open Safari. I can't believe what I'm searching for. There must be something that helps people know whether they're in love or not, right? Maybe it's just the flu.

I click on the first result that pops up and scroll past the introduction until I get to the section 'How to know if you're in love'. This is probably the biggest mistake of my life, and I might need to wash my eyes afterward, but this is better than nothing. I guess.

Taking one more bite of my sugar-bread, I start to read.

· · ·

You notice small things about them.

Like how he hates to wash his hair, the way he watches me in the morning, his obsession with avocados, how he always checks the door twice before leaving, the good amount of cheese he likes on his bread, and how he does his best to be environmentally friendly.

Things that a good friend would probably observe anyway. This doesn't prove anything.

They're all you think about.

Maybe. Yeah. That isn't news to me, though. He and Olivia pretty much invaded my life. Even if I wanted to think about something else, I wouldn't have a chance.

I sigh and drop my head to the countertop. Behind me, the front door opens with a squeak. I straighten up, not expecting anyone, and drag Elias's shirt down over my thighs, since it's the only thing I'm wearing.

Anticipation buzzes over my skin.

The feel of him without actually seeing him is too intense. Just the thought of turning and finding out that it was all in my imagination shreds me apart.

His masculine chuckle echoes behind me. I've never in my life been so happy to hear someone's voice. Goose-bumps cover my skin.

I finally gather the courage to whirl around on the

chair, a shiver running through me. My lips part at the image before me.

"Hi," Elias whispers, looking at me like I'm some kind of hurt puppy.

The dogs run to him, their tails wagging with excitement. He bends down and pets them. Avocado vocalizes his feelings, jumping on him and letting him know between kisses just how much his absence hurt him.

"Hi," I say, my voice cracking and tears filling my eyes.

I run to him, desperate to fall into those strong arms. And I fucking *hate* hugs. He drops his bags and wraps his arms around my waist, lifting me a little before dropping me back down.

He smells so good. I breathe him in. He's here. He's really here. I knew I missed him, but I hadn't realized how much until now.

My hands shake as I grab him tighter, not wanting to let him go, afraid he'll turn around and leave me again.

He kisses my hair and rests his face there for a while, inhaling my scent as I inhale his. He puts his chin on the top of my head, sighing peacefully.

"I've missed you too," he says.

I lean my head back to look at him. He's painfully beautiful. My heart beats like crazy and I know he's looking into my eyes, but mine are roaming over his face, taking in every detail. I press my mouth to his without warning and he kisses me back.

"You're a dick," I huff, smacking my forehead onto his broad chest.

He nods. "Came back with a finished project ready to be sold, though."

"What? What project?" I reply instantly, taking a step back.

Elias smirks, putting his hands in his jeans pockets and rocking on his feet. "Tree therapy will be a real thing by the end of the year."

I gasp at that, knowing how much it means to him. For months, any time I wasn't in his presence, he was locked up in his office, making it all possible. He didn't tell me exactly what he was working on and I didn't ask.

"Holy shit," I say, and he lights up that beautiful grin of his. "But how?"

"Henry Evans and Vanessa Scott finally replied to one of my emails, which explained the idea, and they agreed to meet me. With one condition."

My eyebrows raise in question as I try to process the news. Don't really know who those people are, but by the way he enthuses about them, I bet they're big in the plant industry.

"I have to give them a presentation of all my work. Every bit of research. A body of evidence. Everything I have that could convince them to work with me."

My body relaxes, finally understanding what he's been doing the whole time he was away. Working on something that could change his life in the best way possible.

"You should've told me," I sigh. "I would've been more understanding."

"I wanted it to be a surprise. I wasn't sure if I could finish it in two weeks, so I thought keeping it secret was the best option." Elias shrugs, watching me carefully.

I nod my head in agreement. He's right. I wouldn't have thought less of him if he'd failed to get the presentation done, but he would've felt like he'd disappointed me somehow. Even though that could never be true.

"Do your parents know?"

"Nah," he grimaces, "I've avoided their calls. Couldn't get the image of them crying out of my head."

His expression mirrors how bad he feels. He loved his sister so much and he did his best when it came to being part of her life. Olivia loved him, too. Couldn't stop talking about what a smart brother she had and how lucky she was.

"You should go talk to them. Or at least see them," I suggest, lowering my tone.

"After the meeting, I will."

His gaze flicks behind me, meeting the sketches I've been working on the last three days, all scattered on the kitchen table, along with the meal I was eating before he arrived.

They're not my best, but they're definitely more than I've done in the past few years. When his eyes linger for too long, I lower mine and tug at my T-shirt.

He bypasses me, walking in slow, deliberate steps. Elias grabs them one by one, making sure to analyze every detail until I feel like my soul is standing naked in front of him. Quite intimidating and satisfying at the same time.

"Holy..." he whispers, shuffling through them once more. "These are incredible, Indigo."

I shrug, scratching the back of my neck. The movement lifts the shirt a little over my thighs, but he's too caught up to notice.

"Holy shit. I can't stop staring at them."

Elias lays them all on the countertop, taking another close look. He's seen how I paint, but never how I sketch.

My sketches are so different. They don't have a person or objects as a subject, they're filled with emotions, nothing certain. Just swipes of my pencil, reflecting how I felt in that respective moment.

These are mirroring pain, suffering, home, tiredness, peace. I'd like to make one about love, too.

"Enough about me," I say as he admires my drawings, hands on the edge of the table, muscles flexing. "When's the meeting?"

"Huh?" He turns and looks at his watch. "In fifteen minutes."

"What?" I choke on my own breath.

CHAPTER FORTY FIVE
ELIAS

"THANK YOU, ELIAS." Henry Evans says, sitting up in his office chair and buttoning his jacket. Vanessa Scott does the same in the chair next to him. They look at each other, something passing between them as I sit there, doing my best not to show how nervous I am.

"Why can't I be the one to deliver the news?" Henry stage whispers.

The woman shoots him a look. "Because you did it last time." She gives me a funny smile. "Madden," she starts, and I involuntarily straighten my back and hold my breath. "When can you start?"

My insides explode with happiness, and I don't hear what happens next. I just nod and say *yes* from time to time. I'm imagining everyone's reactions when I tell them the news.

Indigo will be the first to know since she's downstairs in the waiting room. We'll celebrate on our own before going to my parents'. I want to take her home first and—

"Does that work for you?" Henry asks.

I come back to earth. "Sure," I reply calmly, arranging my suit. I feel like I'm about two seconds from fainting. My dream is actually coming true.

"Great. Britt will send the details to your email, and if something isn't right with your place, you can tell us anytime," Vanessa says, smiling up at me like I'm her biggest victory.

"My place?" I tentatively ask.

"Your office down the hall."

Holy cow. My office down the hall? So close to them? Is this a dream? I need someone to pinch me because my entire body is buzzing.

We shake hands, say our goodbyes, and I leave the room, trying not to run or punch the air. Every semblance of dignity goes out of the window as soon as I see Indigo.

When she sees me approach, she jumps to her feet and asks, "You got it?"

I run the last few paces to her, shouting, "Got it!"

She lets out a scream of joy. I've never thought she'd be happy enough to express herself like this in front of other people. I pick her up and carry her like a princess to the car. She squeezes my neck with her slender arms.

"You fucking got it," she says as I lower her into the passenger seat.

She grabs me by my cheeks and kisses me until I'm out of breath. I rub my nose to hers as we break apart.

"Can we go home now before I drag you into the back-seat of the car?"

Indigo nods, biting her lip as I slam the door and rush around to the driver's side. I drive away, and from the corner of my eye, I can see her squeezing her thighs together.

We arrive home in less than two minutes, my hand already in her panties as we enter the house.

My hand presses into her back and she pushes herself into my crotch, stealing a growl from me. I grab the back of her hair and hold her there, gently but firmly, so she has to look into my eyes. After a moment or two, I move down to worship her neck.

With each kiss planted on her, I'm apologizing, trying to make her understand that she's mine. No matter how far I go and no matter how deep I drown.

My hands go for her ass, squeezing it, relishing it. She lets out a moan, pushing herself into me.

"Patience," I whisper in her ear as I pinch one of her nipples through her jacket.

"Fuck patience," she says, knocking my hand aside and unbuttoning her coat and jeans. She looks down hungrily at the bulge in my pants.

She steals a kiss, then throws her clothes on the couch. That earns her a groan, followed by me lifting her up and carrying her to my room, closing the door behind us. I lower her to the bed.

"Stay," I say, taking a step back, wanting to see her in her full glory. "Take your T-shirt off."

She has the sexiest smile on her face as she removes the shirt and her underwear with urgency. My knees go weak under her gaze.

I take off my jeans, my eyes glued to her body. She was brought to Earth to drive me wild with that perfect figure of hers, those lustful and sinful eyes, and the fullest lips on the planet.

I keep my boxers on and stare at her with naked hunger. I've thought about this moment a lot over the last two weeks, pleasuring myself while imagining what I'll do to her.

"Those too," she says, pointing at my last piece of clothing.

Following her orders, my eyes still wander over her body; over her graceful neck that's covered in my kisses, her beautiful breasts with perfect nipples that harden in the hottest way possible. I love the way her curves flow, how she opens her legs for me, teasing me with a filthy look.

This moment has been recreated in my head too many times for it to last only five minutes. Every time we're near each other my hormones go crazy.

My hands grab her feet and pull her down the bed until her ass is close to the edge. I watch her for a couple of painful seconds before opening the drawer behind me and fishing out a condom. I roll it down my hard length.

Kneeling in front of her, my fingers massage the heat between her legs, stimulating it for what comes next. Although, judging by how wet she is, I'd say she's more than ready.

"Elias," she moans as I circle her with the tip of my thumb.

"God, yes," I growl, going faster, hearing her lost in the pleasure.

Her screaming my name does something to me. When she opens her eyes, her pupils are fathomless, filled with arousal.

A hum of satisfaction slips from her lips as I position my tip against her and rub it up and down her folds. She grabs my arm, burying her nails in it. Working her faster, I start to tease her entrance. Without entering, I coat myself in her wetness and my voice grows thick with desire.

She's greedy, spreading her thighs to receive me and my legs shake from the thought of almost being inside her. She whimpers, arching her back and forcing her way onto my shaft. I moan, not resisting the temptation anymore.

"Such an orgasm chaser," I growl, then slam into her.

That's all it takes for her to clench around me, squeezing and teasing me just like I did to her a few moments ago.

I push my full length in and out, trying to get her to finish harder than she's ever done before. I roughly squeeze her cheeks and I keep plunging myself in, over and over. She's so fucking hot, trying to keep those sinful eyes open, head back, lost in the moment.

"Look at me when you come, Indigo," I demand in a husky voice, taking her a little harder. She opens her eyes and I feel her start to shake, tightening around my member.

"I'm gonna come," she moans.

Her stare is so intense. Our moans mix. No more words. Just sounds of pleasure. Clasping her hips, I pull them for a final thrust, my groin tightening in response at the touch of her shaky hands. We shudder, giving in. Friction on friction, pummeling each other to the edge.

I lean forward to touch my forehead to hers, her hot breath brushing my face. Indigo's skin glows with a faint sheen and the floral notes of her perfume hang in the air.

Tracing the delicate softness of her lower lip, I melt into

a kiss that sets fire to my heart. Her mouth opens to me. I lose count of the pecks I cover her in before finally pulling out of her.

She moans in protest, both of us shaking at the loss of body heat. Indigo looks up at me with half-closed eyes and I throw the condom into the trash. I lie down next to her, opening my arms. She falls into them and places her head on my chest, listening to my heartbeat.

We lie like that for a while, neither of us speaking. And it feels good. Indigo is the only person I can bare silence with.

"Olivia was right," I admit.

"About what?" Indigo yawns, her voice cracking.

"About me loving you."

She laughs, covering her face with her hand.

"What?"

"I had to search on Google to see if I love you or not," Indigo says, and I chuckle.

"And?"

"And what?" she groans.

"Have you got your answer?"

"Yup." I raise my eyebrow in question, and she suddenly sobers. "I love you," she declares.

Warmth spreads through me as I catch the tip of her nose between my fingers.

"And I love you, Indigo Hayes."

CHAPTER FORTY SIX

INDIGO

"I WISH YOU WERE HERE," Lorelai whispers. She kneels in front of the gravestone, raises two fingers to her lips, and puts them to Olivia's picture.

Olivia's death changed her a lot. It's been three months since the funeral now, and she's not as happy as she once was. She still smiles, of course, but when she does, her eyes tell a different story.

I know how much it pains Elias to see her like this. His father seems to feel better, though. Whatever his letter said, it made him see things differently. He's not the same as he used to be, but he's trying.

We went to the police a little after Elias came back. Turns out that a couple of other girls had come forward about assaults. That was enough to arrest the school counsellor. He'll spend a long time behind bars, especially as his own daughter will testify at his trial.

None of us are the same, but the months have given us time to grieve and find other things to focus on. Elias has settled into his new job — we barely saw each other for the first month — while I'm planning on opening an online store for my paintings.

Tom started to take darts seriously. He's been invited to a local championship with his teammate. They're rocking it, and I'm sure they'll be stars in no time.

His mom has drowned herself in books, reading one a day. Elias told me he saw her writing in a notebook and I hope she's found a way to express herself. Confessing your thoughts is a great way to heal.

We're not healed, but we're no longer on the bad side of the road, either. All of us took her absence as a motivator to work on ourselves. We think about her when we celebrate, when we fail, and when we get up and start all over again.

"You did an amazing job, Indigo," Lorelai says, getting up from Olivia's grave. She pats my shoulder, looking at me as if I'm an angel.

I asked her a week ago if I could recreate the mural I painted at Elias's place on her gravestone. It took me six days to finish it. Now Tom, Lorelai, Avocado, Dog One and Two are there next to Olivia, Elias, me, and Mushroom.

"Thank you," I say, taking her in my arms. Tom takes this as an invitation and wraps his arms around us, followed by Elias. We do this often.

We told Lorelai and Tom six weeks ago, after things settled a little, that we weren't together to start with. We said how sorry we were and that things between us are more real now than ever. We laid it all out, the whole story. When we finished telling them, Lorelai stretched her hand out to Tom, and Elias and I exchanged confused looks. His father sighed and handed her twenty bucks. She shouted a proud *I told you!*

Turns out she had her suspicions from the beginning. When she saw the two of us on TV at one of my mom's parties, that confirmed it. Tom said there might be an innocent explanation, so they made a bet for twenty bucks.

Our horrific lie was worth twenty whole bucks. I have to admit, we weren't that great at lying. We told them I was from another city and that my parents were dead. So seeing my name on TV, alongside my mother's, made them question our story.

"What do you think she's doing?" Lorelai asks as we break apart.

Elias looks at the sky, smiling. "She's with us."

"Yeah," Tom agrees and bends to kiss her picture.

Elias and I do the same, and we all leave the cemetery in silence.

"Dinner tonight?" Lorelai asks, turning to face us as we reach the parking lot.

"Sure." Elias nods and kisses my head.

I melt under his touch, my head resting on his shoulder as he presses his lips to me one more time.

"See you in a bit," Tom says and places his hand on Lorelai's back, leading her to their car.

"I think she's happy," Elias says as we stop in front of his Mercedes.

"Who? Olivia?" I ask, taking him by the waist.

He looks down at me and gives my nose a peck, then looks back up at the sky, a peaceful smile playing on his lips.

"What makes you think that?" His way of seeing things has always made me curious. I love hearing how the world looks through his eyes.

"Just a feeling." He shrugs, and I playfully bat him on the arm. Elias smirks and looks back to me.

"Tell me."

"I've seen a lot of butterflies lately."

"Me too."

I caught one in my hair the other day, then the next day one flew right in front of my face. We've seen a few on her grave when we've visited as well.

He pulls my body to his as he inhales my scent. "Perfume?" he asks. He seems surprised.

I never use perfume. Only a floral body soap that smells amazing. Didn't think he'd notice. "Yeah."

Elias takes a deep breath. "Smells heavenly."

I still feel weird when he compliments me. I guess I'll have to get used to it since kind words and affection are his love language.

My love language has turned out to be cleaning up after myself, even though I make a huge fuss about it.

Enya says she doesn't have anything to do now. She's lying. I'm cleaning, but I'm not any good at it. She still has a lot to do, and even if I could handle it without her, she's become so important to me. I couldn't imagine my life without her.

It doesn't feel right to say our lives have gotten better in some ways. It's true though. Not because she left, but because her absence has got the best out of us. We're trying our hardest because we know she's watching from above.

I don't want to disappoint her. Or Grandma.

And I won't.

"I love that you don't wear your contacts anymore," Elias says, gazing into my eyes.

I love that he loves my eyes and that he expresses it every chance he has. I love everything about him. I'm not crazy about the weird way he ties his shoes, but I guess I can cope with that for now.

"Unless we try out some roleplay," I tease, poking his chest.

He laughs, throwing his head back. "You and your indigo eyes."

ACKNOWLEDGMENTS

Writing this book has been a challenge. I did it to push my boundaries at first, as English isn't my first language, but writing is in my blood and I figured that it would do no harm to try. And here I am. Publishing my first book.

I'd like to raise my middle finger to those who made me doubt myself and those that said I'd never get here. Ten-year-old me couldn't wait for this moment to come.

Now, to more serious and important things.

There's one person who has stuck beside me, no matter how hard the wind has blown. He's saved me more than once and he's the one who has helped me to heal. My boyfriend has been a rock to me, dealing with my anxiety, depression, and weak moments.

You're the best of me, the reason why I'm breathing easier and lighter. Thank you for always supporting me and making me the person I am today. I love you and thank you for saving me from myself. When you came into my life, your mom helped to ease it all, too. She's one of my biggest supporters and she's shown me love, forcing her way into my heart and warming it whole. I'm so grateful to you two and I couldn't wish for more.

To my sister — thank you for always reading my stories, even when they were on Wattpad and they were total shit. And thank you for my love of tattoos :)

To my bookstagram/booktok angels — thank you for always hyping me up, believing in my dreams, and being there to support me!

Bella, Ellen — thanks to the purest souls on earth. You've been there for me, hyping me from day one when I sent you a snippet of the first thing I'd ever written in English. Love you, girlies xx

Jaclin — thank you for this beautiful interior. I'm obsessed and I know that readers will love it as much as I do. Thank you for making my publishing process easier and for the most beautiful morning texts.

Lily Miller, Marzy Opal — thank you for being there for me! This whole publishing process was hard, but I had the two of you hyping me up with your kind words. I love you.

Anna K. Moss — thank you for helping me see editing from a different perspective. You've made this process a beautiful one and you were there to support me with kind words and wise advice. Are you ready for the next one? xx

To Anca - thank you for being a real one even though we do not speak every day, you are constant in my life and you have supported me through this process since the beginning. We are not cheesy, so let's keep it this way. Thank you xx

ABOUT THE AUTHOR

Maeve Hazel is eighteen years old and she discovered her love of writing when she was little. She loves to eat weird stuff and to argue over things she knows nothing about. She lives with her boyfriend and her two cats, Kit and Mia, who wake her up at six every morning.

New book coming...

Printed in Great Britain
by Amazon

14991211R00150